a modern fairytale

Katy Regnery

The Vixen and the Vet

(Beauty & the Beast)

Never Let You Go

(Hansel & Gretel)

Ginger's Heart

(Little Red Riding Hood)

Dark Sexy Knight

(Camelot)

Don't Speak

(The Little Mermaid)

Shear Heaven

(Rapunzel)

At First Sight

(Aladdin)

At First Sight

a modern fairytale novella

Katy Regnery

AT FIRST SIGHT
Copyright ©2020 by Katharine Gilliam Regnery

Sale of the electronic edition of this book is wholly unauthorized. Except for use in review, the reproduction or utilization of this work in whole or in part, by any means, is forbidden without written permission from the author/publisher.

Katharine Gilliam Regnery, publisher

This book is a work of fiction. Names, characters, places, and incidents are products of the author's imagination or are used fictitiously. Any resemblance to actual events, locales, or persons, living or dead, is entirely coincidental.

All rights reserved, including the right to reproduce this book or portions thereof in any form whatsoever.

Please visit my website at **www.katyregnery.com**

Cover Design: Marianne Nowicki
Developmental Edit: Tessa Shapcott
Line Edit: Ellie McLove
First Edition: June 2020
At First Sight: a novella / by Katy Regnery – 1st ed.
ISBN: 978-1-944810-78-8

To everyone who waited patiently for this story:

Never say never.

Xoxo

PART I:

Fifteen years ago

CHAPTER 1

Fifteen years ago

<u>Ian</u>

"Rake of people here t'night," says one of the extras, banging into me as he rushes off stage.

I grab him by the shoulder. "Full house?"

"Packed. And fancy."

"You see her?"

"Ain't like she's wearin' a feckin' tiara, Ian."

"Huh," I grunt, letting him go and trying to ignore the sudden wave of nerves that thrums through my almost seventeen-year-old body.

Tonight's the final performance—the last time I'll play Mercutio in the Limerick Youth Theatre's production of *Romeo & Juliet*. Because our director—local doctor, Eugene Trímian—updated the play, setting it in the fucking war zone that's modern-day Limerick, we got a big write-up in the Irish News. Some mank limey in London picks up the story and it goes viral in Europe. Suddenly, we start selling out tickets, and now, here we are—with a bunch of randoms from all over the fucking continent filling up the theater on our last night.

And the craic backstage is that there's a princess in the

audience.

A *real* princess.

Honest-to-God royalty visiting from Italy with her parents.

And I can't speak for the other lads, but I wouldn't mind a gawk at her.

Two of my best mates, playing Romeo and Benvolio, line up behind me, ready to go on-stage as soon as Prince Escalus quits yelling at the Capulets and Montagues.

"Jack Murphy said he saw her arrive in a limo. Said she's deadly," whispers my friend, Sean.

"Jack Murphy can feck off," says Luke. "Face like chewed toffee."

In Limerick, you know who you are early, and you're either for Keegan-Clancy or for Murphy-Doyle. Seeing as how my mother was a Keegan by birth, I got recruited young. Same with Sean and Luke. We all came up Keegan-Clancy together, but we'll be lucky if we live to see twenty with the way tensions are on the street.

That was the whole point of this play, in fact: to give hooligans like myself, aligned with Limerick gangs from the cradle, the chance to act in a theatrical production on neutral territory. Me and my lads got cast as the Montagues. Them from Murphy-Doyle play the Capulets. But the catch is that there was no fighting allowed while we were at rehearsals. No grudges in the theater. Didn't think it would work out, but somehow it did. We stayed civil with each other for a whole six weeks of summer rehearsals, and I won't lie, I even started to like a few of those Murphy-Doyle bastards while we learned lines and blocking and theater-style sword-fighting. Even Jack Murphy, who I was raised to hate, ain't all that bad…especially when he plays Tybalt and you get to watch him die at every rehearsal.

That said, if there's a princess here tonight, she ain't going off with Jack Murphy. If she's going off with anyone, it'll be me. But first, I gotta see her.

"That's our cue," says Sean, who plays Romeo.

I step out on stage in my black t-shirt and tight jeans, my eyes adjusting to the bright lights as I lean against a *papier-mache* tree and eavesdrop on my co-stars talking about a Capulet bird named Rosaline.

"Ah, me," sighs Sean, his Limerick accent thick over Shakespeare's lines. "Sad hours seem long…"

"What sadness lengthens Romeo's hours?" asks Luke in his monotone robot voice. I roll my eyes. Scrappy as fuck, Luke's the best brawler I ever met, but he couldn't act his way out of a paper sack and that's the truth of it.

I don't have any lines until scene four, so I ignore the pair of them and scan the audience, my eyes landing on familiar faces: Mary Murphy, mother of pizza-faced Jack, sits in the middle of the third row like she's the bloody queen of Éire. Behind her is Horatio Doyle, an up-and-comer in Murphy-Doyle, with a few of his lads flanking him. Two rows behind them, I can make out the dark, beady eyes of my cousin, Jarlath Keegan.

It was Jarlath what first got me and my little brother running with the Keegans, promising us hot dinners while me mam was high as a kite. She was chewed up and spit out by my twelfth birthday, and Jarlath—ten years older than me—ended up taking in me and nine-year-old Albie. He used to beat us on the regular too, but over the last three years, I got bigger and started fighting back. I know he still gets a punch in on Albie from time-to-time, but not if I'm around. He don't dare hit the kid in front of me. I'm a mean, whatever-it-takes, street-rat style fighter, just like he taught me to be. And what I lack in muscle tone I make up for in grit. I don't stop hitting until my enemy is down for good.

We lock eyes for a second, my cousin and me, with him putting a tattooed arm around my brother's scrawny shoulders just to rattle me. Albie don't notice. He's focused on the action up on stage. I narrow my eyes, warning my cousin to leave Albie the fuck alone, and he winks at me with a lazy smirk on his ugly gob. I fucking hate him, I do.

Skimming my eyes away, I look for...for...

Her.

Fuck me.

Her.

I barely notice that my fingers are curling into fists, but they are, and while they're at it, my heart speeds up, galloping like a pony at the track.

Ka-dum. Ka-dum. Ka-dum. Ka-dum.

The muscles in my chest flex and harden as I breathe deep and hold it. I step away from the tree, straightening up a little and focusing my eyes on the white-blonde of her hair—on the way the stream of a spotlight from the back of the theater tosses a halo over her head.

A *halo*.

Like she's a fucking angel. Like she's legendary. Like she's not even real.

Princess.

There's no mistaking *who* she is or *what* she is—it's clear in the way she holds herself, sitting in a rickety velvet seat that's seen better days: back straight, neck long, little chin tilted up, and wide, dark eyes fixed on the stage.

Princess.

My head tilts to the left and my face falls slack as I stare at her, eyes like fucking lasers, riveted on her beautiful face.

I'm sure her skin is a regular pinkish color up close, but from here, with that glaring spotlight and from a bit of a distance, she's almost otherworldly. Her crisp white shirt is open at the neck and a string of pearls hugs the base of her throat. Her light hair falls behind her shoulders in white waves, and tiny white sparkles in her ear lobes draw my eyes. I imagine the softness of that skin against my lips, compressed between my teeth. My filthy mouth waters as I slide my gaze to her mouth. Full and soft, her lips are a high-tone glossy in the light that streams over her head. A mental image of them wrapped around my cock makes my balls tighten.

Make no mistake: I ain't lonely. I get it on the regular when I want it, and mostly with who I choose, but suddenly I feel like a green kid who's never fucked.

That's about when I realize I'm wearing tight jeans.

On a stage.

In front of the whole of Limerick.

I tear my eyes away from her and stare down, expecting to see my cock rising like the River Shannon in high tide.

Sheep. Tea. Rugby. Cricket. Limey bastards. The Queen of bloody England with her thousand-year-old cunt.

I purse my lips together and breathe slowly through my nose, thinking of everything I hate, trying to get that beautiful fucking image out of my head before I'm sporting an on-stage boner. And thank the good Lord above for small mercies, but I feel my blood recede before the audience notices my struggle, except…

Except when I glance up again, *she's* looking at me. *Right* at me.

Her.

Princess.

Seemingly aware of my struggle, and definitely amused, she fights not to smile as she lowers her gaze to my cock for a long second, then skims it back up my body to nab my eyes again.

Brazen as fuck she is!

Locked with hers, I feel my own eyes widen with disapproval as hers sparkle with laughter.

Laughter! Laughter?

Looking away from her, to a spot on the back wall of the theater, I make my face into stone. Fuck her and her fucking laughter. Ain't had no fucking complaints in bed yet, and certainly no fucking laughter.

Unable to stop myself, I slide my eyes back to hers and watch as she straightens her lips, lifting her head a touch and shifting her gaze to the stage. Now, she's haughty.

Yeah, I think. *That's right, princess. I'm no feckin' joke.*

But not a moment later, her eyes slip back to mine, and this time—if I'm not mistaken—there's a question in them. Or a challenge? Hmm.

Wide and sharp, they lock with mine in a hot look, daring me to…to…—*Jaysus, Mary and Joseph*—I don't know. I don't fucking know. Not a fucking surprise, but I don't speak princess very fucking well.

All I know is that she's asking me *for* something. I just don't know what.

What do you want? I wonder, wishing I could jump off this fucking stage, climb over all the people between me and her, clasp her perfect face in my dirty hands, and ask her.

"I'll go along, no such sight to be shown. But to rejoice in splendor of mine own," says Romeo.

And then the stage goes dark.

***

Valentina

Che palle!

What balls!

Indignance is mandatory, of course, because no one is allowed to look at me like that. I *must* be insulted that he'd be so bold, some young actor in a third-rate Irish play…but I can't help the smile that blooms across my face while the stage crew changes the set for the next scene.

Tall. Muscular. Dark hair. Navy blue eyes.

Black Irish.

He was wearing makeup on his face, but it didn't hide the scar on his left cheek, and nothing on God's green earth could quell the simmering intensity in his eyes.

Dio mio! Scrappy, coarse and brutish, I was drawn to him the moment he walked out on stage.

Before he noticed me, I noticed him, standing against that tree with an insouciance better left to royalty. As he scanned the audience, the muscles in my stomach coiled tighter and tighter, wondering when and if his searing gaze would land on me. His eyes rested first on an older lady, narrowing with disgust, and I could feel his disdain of her to my very core. Finding him far more compelling than the amateur acting on-stage, I followed his eyes as they slid to the man seated behind the woman, and then to the tall man and teenager sitting just in front of me.

The tall man had leered at me when I sat down before the play, licking his lips in a way so darkly suggestive, previous generations of De'Medicis would have answered such insolence with poison. Maybe I felt a kinship to the young actor when I noted his reaction to the man—a look of such contempt, I felt like my honor had been somehow restored.

And that was the moment his eyes slipped to mine.

I watched his fingers fist and his eyes widen; the way his body straightened, and his chest swelled. For me. *All* for me.

I didn't miss the swelling of something else either, though he stared at the floor with intense concentration until the growing bulge in his tight jeans stopped rising. A fever spread out over my skin as I watched his struggle.

Why'd you get so mad? I wonder as the lights come up on the second or third scene of the play. Wait. Fourth? I can't remember. I've been ignoring the poorly acted play, glancing up for the sole purpose of scanning the stage for him before losing myself in my own thoughts. But this time…when I look up…he's back.

He enters with several other actors, including the ones playing Romeo and Benvolio, and I hold my breath, waiting for him to speak. When he does, I melt.

"*You are a lover,*" he says, "*borrow Cupid's wings.*"

His voice is low and gravelly, with a grim color and gritty timbre. It's older than he looks, like it's been used a lot longer than sixteen or seventeen years. Like it maybe screamed itself into hoarseness at some point and never recovered.

He cheats his body toward the audience as he speaks his next line, finding my face and nailing me with his eyes: "*If love be rough with you, be rough with love.*"

I gasp softly at the combination of threat and promise in his delivery; at the way my flesh prickles and breath catches.

"*I dreamed a dream tonight,*" says Romeo.

"*And so did I,*" answers my dark Mercutio.

"*Well, what was yours?*"

I am on the edge of my seat when he grabs my eyes again. "*That dreamers often lie.*"

"*Non guardare*," my mother whispers close to my ear. *Look away.*

I jump a touch, startled by her sharp whisper and annoyed by her command.

"*Perché?*" I murmur. *Why?*

She narrows her eyes at me, and I huff softly, angling my body away from her and averting my eyes from Mercutio, who is in the middle of a monologued tirade.

My mother can demand that I observe propriety, but she cannot force me to stop listening to his voice. And though he speaks too quickly for me to understand all of his accented English, I don't need the words. I hear the passion in his voice. I hear the anger in it when I am no longer watching him. And I know it's directed at me.

Though we have never met one another, I feel like we are somehow connected, this young actor and I, and wonder if he feels it too. It's thrilling to be silently bound to him like this—to this barbarian Irishman who, according to the newspaper, is probably part of a street gang.

My mother was against my twin brother and I attending the theater tonight, but after reading an article about the way the show was fostering friendships between rival gangs, my father insisted on our presence, telling her that Nico and I were too sheltered for our own good.

"They are spoiled children who don't understand the plight of the common man!" he'd thundered. "Pampered royals who don't know what other children suffer."

"You *want* your children to suffer?" my mother had screamed back.

"I want them to know that their lives are not normal."

"And gang fighting is *normal*? You want to see it glamorized on stage?"

"We are *Italian*!" he'd yelled, his eyes popping out of his head. "The birthplace of *mafia*."

"We are *royalty*," she'd answered, eyeing him with disgust. "Above such things."

"We may *live* above such things," he'd conceded with finality, "but we have a responsibility not to ignore them. Nico and Tina will attend the play…and that's final."

Having spent most of our evenings bored to death in elegant hotels since beginning this European tour, Nico had grinned at me once we were alone in our room.

"An evening at the theater, eh?"

"Ha!" I'd chortled, falling back dramatically on the bed. "*La Scala* is the theater. This is…a joke. Street urchins playing at Shakespeare. Ugh."

"You're such a snob, Tina."

"*Va bene.* I'm a snob. I can live with that, brother."

"It *might* be good."

"Un-bloody-likely," I'd answered, stealing one of England's more colorful phrases.

But now? Listening to the mesmerizing voice of this *un-bloody-likely* Mercutio, I don't feel like a snob at all. I feel vulnerable. I feel…alive.

Moreover, I know—by her long-suffering and annoyingly loud sighs—that my mother will fall asleep in the next ten to fifteen minutes…which means that I can spend the rest of the play blatantly ogling handsome, dangerous Mercutio to my heart's bloody content.

CHAPTER 2

<u>Valentina</u>

I was right, of course.

My mother was asleep by scene six, which left me free to watch my Mercutio with unfettered abandon. And something inside of me—in addition to my abominable snobbery—died with him as he perished on stage. I'm fairly certain it was the last of my reservations:

I *must* meet him.

As the actors bow, I whisper to my brother.

"Nico," I say, tossing a quick glance at my mother, who is just starting to rouse herself from sleep amid thunderous applause. "I'm going out tonight."

"No, you're not," says my brother.

"Yes. I am."

"Nope. Not allowed."

I roll my eyes at him. *My twin, the rule follower.*

"I'm going out," I repeat, "and you're going to cover for me."

"Wrong again."

I ignore him, laying out the lie I want him to tell. "Tell them I was invited to a party by a—a school friend. Tell them I took Gaspare."

"Gaspare's back at the hotel with the flu," says Nico.

He's right. Unfortunately, my bodyguard's been down for the count since we arrived in Ireland, leaving Nico's bodyguard, Iago, to look after us both on his own.

"You'll say he had a miraculous recovery. Tell them he showed up in the back of the theater and agreed to take me to a party."

"When did you get invited to a party, Tina? You don't know anyone in Ireland!"

"Don't worry about it." I lean down and grab my purse. "Just cover for me."

"This town isn't safe," he whispers, darting a glance at my mother, who is rubbing her eyes and yawning. She's going to stand up and join in the applause in a second, and once she's awake, I'll miss my window to escape. I need to get going. Now.

"Don't ruin this for me, Nic," I snarl. "I'm going out with your help or not!"

He stares at me, his eyes boring into mine, and for a second I think he'll say no, but then he nods once, even though misgivings flood his narrowed eyes. "Fine. When will you be back?"

"Later," I whisper, stepping over him and sliding my way out of the row and up the aisle to a door marked exit in the back corner of the theater.

I push it open and as it clicks shut behind me, I realize I'm not in front of the theater under a well-lit marquee, but in a dark, narrow alleyway adjacent to the theater building. For a second, I let my eyes adjust to the light from a cobwebbed bulb over my head, looking to my left and right to find myself utterly alone except for a yellow-eyed cat who eyes me from atop a pungent dumpster. The painted words "STAGE ENTRANCE" on a rusty door beside the dumpster, tells me exactly where I am.

If I wait here, I think, my heart pounding with anticipation, *he'll come out of that door and I'll get to meet him.*

My skin prickles and I release a shaky breath as I recall the intensity of his gaze from on-stage.

It's not that I've lived an entirely sheltered life where men are concerned. I'm fifteen, after all—I've had my share of stolen kisses and copped feels, especially at royal weddings when my mother is distracted by her friends and I can sneak into a dark garden with a handsome boy. That said, however—as is expected for one of my rank and status—my virginity is intact, and expected to remain so until I marry.

At the end of the alleyway, I notice theatergoers pouring onto the sidewalk, and I move to the wall opposite the stage door, out of the light. I don't lean against the filthy concrete wall behind me, but I do fold my arms under my breasts, which gives me a little extra cleavage in the V-neck of my white silk blouse. Super skinny midnight-blue jeans and open-toed, four-inch, fire-engine-red heels round out my ensemble. Casual for home. Not for Limerick. And not ideal for a cobblestoned alley.

What if he has a girlfriend?

The question slides through my head like a bad dream,

and I pull the leather backpack off my back, rooting around for a cigarette.

If he does, you'll look like an idiot, standing here alone, waiting for him like a groupie.

I light the tobacco and breathe deeply.

Your parents are going to be furious. This is stupid. You should go.

I exhale, watching the smoke curl up to the sky, feeling my misgivings grow with every passing second while I wait in limbo for Mercutio's arrival.

Forget this boy. Walk back to the Palace Hotel and slip into bed before they realize you're gone.

But just as I'm about to turn around, I hear voices from inside, approaching the stage door. Young men. Laughing and talking.

He's coming!

I throw the cigarette on the ground and stamp it out with my toe just as the door opens and three young actors pour out into the narrow space. A quick scan confirms that none of them is my Mercutio.

"Hey, now. What's this?"

A tall blonde boy, who played Tybalt in the play, looks me up and down, stepping closer. His friends stand behind him; out of deference to him or me?—I'm not sure.

"Yer the princess," he says, clamping his eyes on my chest before skimming them up slowly to check out my face.

"Princess. *Sí*," I say, uncrossing my arms and lifting my chin as I glance over his shoulder. The door doesn't magically open to reveal Mercutio, however, so I meet the blonde boy's eyes again. "*Sono*—I mean, I am Her Serene Highness Valentina Yasmina De'Medici."

"La-ti-da! Lads," he says slowly, licking his lips, "we got us a real live princess here."

There's such unmasked menace in his voice, the hairs on the back of my neck stand up.

Without actually meaning to, I take a step back, but there's nowhere to go. The fine fabric of my white blouse presses against the dank, damp concrete behind me.

He leans forward, placing his palms flat on the wall behind me so that I'm bracketed by his arms. "Why're you here in an alley all by yer lonesome? What d'you want, Princess? Who're you waitin' for?"

He wouldn't actually do anything to me, would he? No. No! He knows who I am. He's just trying to impress his friends.

"I wait for…s-someone," I say, my English abandoning me as my confidence wanes.

"She waits for…*someone*." He mimics my strong Italian accent, smirking over his shoulder at his "lads."

"I think," he says, leaning forward to press his forehead to mine, "ye're waitin' for me."

"*Non*." I struggle to escape under his arm, but he grabs my shoulders and shoves me back against the wall.

"Yer not goin' anywhere, Princess. Not until I taste some royal honey."

Panic.

My heart rate soars, beating like a bass drum in my ears; so loud, I'm sure he can hear it.

My eyes skitter to the mouth of the alley, where the crowd has thinned, but some audience members still linger. It's got to be about fifteen meters away, though, and the distance, combined with street cacophony, means that no one would hear me if I screamed. Anyway, he could have his hand clamped over my mouth and my shirt torn open in the time it would take to fill my lungs with enough air.

"*Per favore.* P-Please," I say, my voice thin and frightened. "Please let me...ah, let me to go now."

"Go?" he asks, shaking his head slowly. "Nah. I don't think so."

He leans closer and opens his mouth. I close my eyes and cringe as his tongue, wide and wet, lands on my jawbone and licks a leisurely path to my ear.

"Feckin' sweet," he sighs.

I'm so terrified of what's coming next, I feel lightheaded. I've got to do *something*. Bracing my palms flat on the wall behind me, I bring my knee up as fast and hard as possible. Because he's still standing so close to me, it connects hard with his groin, and I feel his hands slip from my shoulders as he stumbles backward into his friends.

"Fuck! Ya mangy feckin' bitch!" he bellows, reaching for his balls as the stage door opens again.

"What the fuck is this?"

Still standing with my back against the wall, I raise my eyes to Mercutio's, and above the bodies between us, our eyes lock just as they did inside the theater. And despite the blonde boy's menacing words and how close I likely came to something infinitely uglier than being licked on the cheek, I feel myself relax. I can't say why, but just seeing Mercutio so close to me makes me feel a relief so strong and so sure, I slump a little against the wall and my eyes fill with tears of relief.

"Princess," he says softly, stepping into the crowded alley with the actors who played Romeo and Benvolio. As the door clicks shut behind them, he darts a glance at the groaning blonde boy still cupping his groin, then at me, then back at the boy. His eyes narrow. "What happened here? What'd you do, Jack Murphy? What the fuck did you do to her? I'll kill you if you hurt her!"

"Fuck you," he chokes out. "Fuck you and fuck yer dead Keegan crackhead mam."

Mercutio doesn't react to this, but he turns to me, his eyes blazing and fierce. "He…touched you?"

I gulp softly, blinking back the tears in my eyes as I cast my gaze down.

"You bottom-feedin' piece of shite." He turns to his friends, cracking his knuckles as he barks out, "Get her outta here. I'll find ya's."

Romeo offers me his hand and I take it, letting him and Benvolio lead me quickly out of the alley. The sound of fighting—of skin landing violently against skin—echoes against the stone and concrete behind me.

"You should…to help him!" I say, trying to look over my shoulder at the three-on-one fight commencing behind me.

"*Help* him?" asks Romeo. He chuckles. "Nah. Jack's

nuts is now in his throat, thanks to you, and the other two is little. Ian's gotcha."

"You are…Ian?" I ask.

"Nah. Ian's the one back there…fightin' fer yer royal honor."

"Ian," I say softly. Mercutio's name is Ian.

"Yeah. Ian. Ian Ladd is him. I'm Sean. Yer man on the other side is Luke. And yer…?"

"Valentina," I say. "T-Tina."

"Well, Tina, it's good t'meecha. Jack Murphy's a right bastard. It's good we come along when we did."

"*Sí*," I say, surprised to find I'm still holding hands with Sean as we turn right onto the sidewalk and stop in front of a coffee shop. I pull my hand away and clear my throat, looking through the large plate glass window into the warm café. I'm about to cry and I'd prefer not to have an audience. "I need, ah…the toilet."

"Yeah," says Sean. "Sure. You go on in. We'll be waitin' here when you come out."

"Th-Thank you," I manage to whisper, slipping into the shop just as my tears begin to fall.

In the ladies' room, I scrub that animal's saliva off my face, splash my cheeks with water and fix my makeup as best I can. As soon as I thank Mercutio for his assistance, I'll call the hotel and have them send a car to collect me. This has all been a massive mistake.

There's no sign of Sean or Luke as I make my way back through the bustling cafe, but Mercu—*Ian* is sitting at a two-chair table by the front window, a cup of tea in front of him and another at the vacant place across from him.

For me? He looks up as I approach, his eyes widening, flicking to the cup and then back to my face. *Yes, for you.*

"May I join you?" I ask, waiting for him to stand up and help me sit. The least I can do is thank him for his assistance before leaving.

"Obviously," he says, gesturing to the empty chair with an outstretched hand. His knuckles are cracked and bloody, and I cringe, sucking in a sharp breath. It's *my* fault he was hurt. I never should have been in that alley alone. My parents are always reminding me of how reckless I am, but tonight I *feel* it. And I hate it that Ian has been hurt because of me.

Pulling out my own chair, I try for a smile. "I'm sorry...for your hands."

He looks at my face, searching it like he doesn't know what I'm talking about. I reach out, gingerly touching the backs of his fingers. "You're, um, bleeding."

As I touch him, I hear a hitch in his breathing. "It's—it's nothin'."

"I'm sorry."

"Ain't yer fault," he insists, sliding his hand away and holding it up to inspect the damage. After a moment, he shrugs, flattening the hand on the table again. "Besides...it was worth it."

I gulp. "I don't know what would happen...if you didn't come along."

"You got him pretty good, I guess," Ian says, a glimmer of admiration in his eyes as he lifts his cup to blow on the steaming tea.

As I watch his lips purse, I realize he hasn't got a fresh scratch or bruise on his face. The three boys in the alley didn't land one punch.

"I think you got him better," I say.

"Then we're a good team," he tells me, his gaze soft and thoughtful as he scans my face.

I hold out my hand. "I'm—"

"Tina. I heard."

"Valentina, actually."

"Heard that too."

"I'm a—"

"Princess."

"Yes."

"From Italy."

"*Sì*. I mean, yes. You know a lot about me."

"We heard you lot were comin' to the show tonight." He grins at me again and he's so damn handsome, my heart flip flops. "What'd you think? Of the play?"

"Better than I expected," I answer honestly.

"You expected shite?"

He scoffs, running a hand through his thick, black hair. One lock won't comply and falls back onto his forehead rebelliously. Oh, how I long to tame that unruly curl—to feel its softness between my fingers as I push it back into the fold.

My eyes widen as I realize he's frowning at me. "Sh-shite?"

"Shit."

I sit up straighter, a little surprised he'd use such vulgar language with me.

"*Shit*," he repeats, a roguish grin teasing the edges of his mouth. "Caca. Crap. Poo—"

"Yes, thank you, I know…*shit*." I pick up my cup and take a sip of the strong, black, Irish tea. "Your show was *not* shit. It wasn't *that* bad. *You* weren't bad. *You* were quite good, in fact."

He leans his elbows on the table, his dark blue eyes capturing mine and his lips widening into a smile. "You think so?"

I nod, utterly charmed by him, still in awe of the fact that he took on those three ruffians to save me. "I think so. *Sí*. Yes."

"*Sí*. Hmm." He tilts his head to the side, holding my eyes as his narrow a touch. "What are you doin' tonight, Valentina De'Medici?"

Calling a car and going back to my hotel.

That's what I *should* say. What I end up saying, however, is…

"Nothing, I think." My eyes drop to my tea, thinking there will be absolute hell to pay when I return to my hotel later. "Sipping t-tea with you, for now."

"And after that?"

A knock on the window makes us both look up. For the first time, I realize that Sean and Luke have been standing guard outside of the café while Ian and I have been sitting together inside. Sean hooks his thumb to the right and raises his eyebrows.

Ian looks back at me. "Don't move. I'll be right back, yeah?"

"Okay."

I watch him stand up, his body tall and muscular in jeans and a t-shirt. The door jingles cheerfully as he steps outside to speak with his friends. They huddle together in a small circle, their faces intense and unhappy as Luke and Sean take turns talking. Finally, Ian stands up straight and puts his hands on his hips, twisting his head just a touch to look at me before turning back to his friends. A few words are exchanged, and then Luke and Sean are off, walking quickly to the left, out of my line-of-sight.

When Ian sits back down across from me, his eyes are heavy.

"Is everything...okay?" I ask him.

"Those Murphy bastards? What were botherin' you? They're gettin' pissed down the street. Shootin' their mouths off 'bout what happened in the alley."

A tremor of fear runs through me, and I push away from the table, standing up. I have no interest in renewing my acquaintance with Jack Murphy. "I should go. G-Go back to my hotel."

Ian is up in a flash, standing across from me. "If you have to go, I'll take you. No harm will come to you if you're with me, I promise."

His eyes are stormy and hard, like he's seen immeasurable sadness in his short life, but his eyelashes are jet black and insanely long. They soften his expression;

soften the fury that simmers in his eyes.

"I don't want you to get hurt again," I say. "Not for me."

"Princess," he says, the "r" rolling softly on his Irish tongue, "I'd take fifty t'ousand beatin's for a single evenin' with you."

O cuore mio. How can I resist this boy?

"Where can we go?" I ask him. "To escape these…Murphy bastards?"

He laughs when I swear, then asks, "Do ya trust me, Tina?"

Dio mio, I know I shouldn't. There is no good reason for me to trust this Irish street boy, and every reason why I shouldn't. He is poor and dirty. He fights with his hands like a brute and looks at me like I'm a snack.

But would he save me from harm only to hurt me himself? Would he be my savior only to defile me later? No. He wouldn't. Something inside of me knows he wouldn't.

"*Sí,*" I say. "I trust you, Ian."

He reaches for my hand, and I giggle as he pulls me out of the café.

CHAPTER 3

Valentina

Hours later, as we approach the Limerick Palace Hotel hand in hand, I wonder at the whole new world I've discovered tonight by moonlight: parks and cathedrals, rivers and mountains, castles and gardens.

The city I'd originally regarded as shabby has become the jewel in Ireland's crown.

I also wonder if it's possible to fall in love so fast, over the course of the last few precious hours; cherished minutes when I was just Tina, an Italian girl visiting Ireland, who found her handsome champion in a dark alley, and felt more in one night than she'd felt in her entire life up to now.

I cannot be the same person I was when I walked into that theater tonight.

It's impossible.

I feel completely new.

In the People's Park he took me to a red and white gazebo where we danced to a melody floating on the breeze, like the young lovers in *The Sound of Music*.

On Mathew's Bridge he put his arms around me from behind and brushed his lips along the back of my neck, murmuring my name—*Tina...Tina...Tina*—like he was drunk from the sound of it.

In a shadowed corner of St. Mary's Cathedral, he stole a kiss from me: a quick peck on the lips after we'd each lit a candle.

And with the medieval towers of King John's Castle looming behind us, he drew me into his arms and kissed me like a man kisses a woman he loves: with our bodies pressed intimately together and his tongue sliding like satin against mine.

A fitting place for a royal princess to lose her heart to a street punk: in the shadow of a castle.

And now, hand in hand, as every ancient clock in this city chimes three, we approach the Limerick Palace Hotel where my family is staying.

My heart is in my throat because I don't want to say goodnight or goodbye to Ian. I want every possible second with my hand in his, my mouth pressed against his, my body doing things with his that are forbidden. For the first time in my life, I know what desire is, and it's a feeling so sharp and intense, I've never known its equal. I want more. So much more.

"Don't look now," he says, pulling me sharply against his side and stopping abruptly on the sidewalk half a block from my hotel. "But that's a whole lot of coppers, Tina."

Dio Mio! Blue and red lights blink wildly, reflecting garishly off the massive, white marble hotel. "Surely that's not…"

The words die on my lips. A princess has gone missing.

And my parents have called out the local cavalry to find me.

"For you?" asks Ian, pulling me into the shadow afforded by a cafe's dark doorway. "I'm certain, love, that's exactly why they're here."

I look up at him, into the face of the young man who's been the center of my world tonight. "What should we do?"

"I have an idea." Ian reaches in his back pocket and pulls out his phone. "I know one of the maids who works there."

"How well?" I ask, unable to keep the jealousy out of my voice.

He smirks at me. "Not *that* well."

Somewhat mollified, I cross my fingers, hoping she's working tonight.

"Mollie!" He grins at me as he presses the phone against his ear. "Yeah. Yeah. Aw, shite. Ye're a ball buster, woman." He shakes his head and chuckles. "I need a favor." Cringing as she answers, he follows up with, "C'mon, Mol. Never promised you nothin', love."

I look down at my aching feet, realizing that they haven't bothered me until now. I was walking on clouds until Ian called this—this…*Mollie*.

As if sensing my mood, his arm snakes around my waist and he pulls me closer. When I look up, into his eyes, they search mine. After a moment, he grins at me and kisses my forehead.

"Sneak me and a friend through the kitchen to the service elevator, yeah?" I can't hear Mollie's exact response, but from Ian's grimace, I gather it isn't especially encouraging. "Please, love. I'll never ask for anythin' ever again, yeah?" I feel him hold his breath—the way his inflated lungs push against mine as he waits for her response. Finally he exhales. "Thanks, Mol! See you soon."

He pockets the phone and puts his other arm around my waist, holding me tightly against his body in the narrow doorway. A wicked grin lifts his lips.

"Ye're jealous."

"Who's Mollie?" I demand.

He drops his lips to mine and my mouth opens instantly, helpless to resist him. Lingering on my lips, I can feel another part of him prodding my belly. He's hard for me, and I can't lie. It's thrilling.

"Come on," he says, grabbing my hand and walking us back out onto the sidewalk.

We cross to the opposite side of the street, quickly pass by the hoopla at the front entrance, and cross back over, making our way down an alley. Ian knocks on a nondescript door twice, and it opens to reveal a young woman in a dark green and white hotel maid uniform.

"Yer gonna get me fired, Ian Ladd," she hisses, checking me out as we slip inside. "Who's this, now?"

"Tina, this is Mollie. Mollie, this is Tina."

Her eyes widen in recognition. "Fuck, Ian. It's the—her highness—the princess—oh, shite! *You* kidnapped the princess?"

"I was not *kid*-napped," I say, lifting my chin so I can look down at this Mollie.

"But the hotel said—"

Ian chuckles beside me. "Me and Tina's just been seein' the sights."

"*Tina?* Jaysus, Mary and Joseph, yer gonna get yerself arrested, Ian, you thick eejit."

He leans forward to press his lips on her fat cheek, and I stiffen beside him. If I was the princess of Ireland, I'd have this woman beheaded *presto*.

"Nah. I'm lucky and you know it."

"Luck runs out, ya mad bastard," says Mollie, flicking a nervous glance at me.

"We'll get outta yer hair," says Ian, tugging on my hand to pull me down the dim hallway. "I know the way. Mum's the word, Mol."

As we leave *Mollie* by the service entrance and race through the basement hallways of the old hotel, I giggle like Kate Winslet in *Titanic*, glorying in the feeling of Ian holding my hand tightly and hosting me to this wild night. I wouldn't give up a moment of it for all the world.

"How do you know your way around?" I ask him when we stop in front of a battered elevator.

"My mam—and Mollie's, for that matter—worked here when we were small. We ran around these halls together for hours." The door slides open. "What floor are you on?"

"Fifteen." I step into the lift beside him. "What's the plan?"

"To sneak you back into your room."

"Is that possible?"

He plants a kiss on the tip of my nose. "These old

hotels have service corridors where maids and valets could slip in and out of rooms unseen."

"Do I want to know the sort of mischief this led to when you and Mollie were small?"

He grins at me, shaking his head. "Nope."

"So we will…slip back into my room?'

"That's the plan," he says, a shadow passing over his face as he looks down at me.

My heart squeezes. *I don't want to say goodbye either.*

When the lift stops, he pulls me into another dimly-lit service hallway. As we walk down the carpeted corridor, I realize that there are brass plaques on the plain white doors: *1501 Bedroom #1, 1501 Living Room*, etc.

"What suite are you in?" he whispers.

"1506," I say.

"We'll have to guess which bedroom," he says. "There are two, if memory serves."

"One's mine and one is Nico's."

"Will Nico rat us out if you get it wrong and walk into his?" he asks.

I shake my head. "I don't think so."

1504 Bedroom #2…1505 Pantry…1505 Bedroom #1…

I squeeze Ian's hand. "What if—"

He pauses in his long strides, turning around to look at me. "What?"

"I don't want you to go," I whisper, looking up at his handsome face. I reach up to trace the scar on his cheek with my fingertip, my body swaying into his. "Stay."

"*Princess*," he murmurs, putting his arms around me. He bites his bottom lip then lets it go. "How? There are going to be cops in there, hotel people, your parents—"

I glance at the door that reads: *1506 Bedroom #1*. "Give me fifteen minutes to get rid of them. Wait in the hall. If I knock on the door, you can come in. If I don't…"

He takes a deep breath and lets it go slowly. "Then this is goodbye."

"It's not," I say. *I refuse to say goodbye to him.* "Wait here."

Turning the knob, I slip into the dark bedroom, relieved to discover it's mine, not Nico's. No one is waiting for me inside the room, though I can hear voices in the shared living room area just beyond the double doors. Quickly undressing, I throw my nightgown over my head and pull my hair into a ponytail. I consider messing up the bed, but decide on a different tactic instead. Tiptoeing to the armoire, I take the extra pillow and blanket from the top shelf and make a messy bed for myself on the small chaise lounge in the corner of the dressing room.

I squint my eyes as I would if I was awoken from a deep sleep, then walk through the double doors into Nico's and my shared living area.

Several Irish police officers scurry about while my parents' security team, including Gaspare and Iago, sit on the couch, their heads together in conversation as my mother weeps quietly. Nico sees me first. His face registers surprise, then relief, then fury.

"Where the *hell* have you been?" he cries, rushing across

the room.

I fake a yawn, scratching a nonexistent itch on my shoulder. "What's…going on?"

He hugs me close, whispering in my ear, "You are in so…much…trouble."

"We'll see," I mumble back, pushing him away.

"Valentina!" shrieks my mother. "Where have you been?"

She leaps up from the couch with my father right behind her.

"*Dio Mio*, Valentina!" he exclaims. "We were so worried!"

"Uh…the princess has been found. I repeat: the princess has been found," says one of the police officers into his radio.

As my mother envelops me in her perfumed embrace, I fake-yawn again. "What in the world is going on?"

"You were missing!" yells my father.

"I was asleep," I say, blinking like I've just woken up. I gesture to my room. "You don't believe me? Look."

My parents hustle into my room and turn on the light to find my bed still freshly made. "Your bed doesn't have a wrinkle!"

"Not *there*," I say with a long-suffering sigh. I point to the dressing room, where the small, antique chaise sits overlooked in the far corner. "*There*."

Nico leans against the doorway to my room, watching us with annoyance. "I thought you were going to a party."

"I went. I came back. I fell asleep," I say, looking at all of them like they're crazy.

"Madame, sir, is everything in order?" The hotel concierge stands beside my brother, wringing his hands.

"*Va bene*," says my mother, waving him away. "She's been here all along. We were worried for nothing."

"What a relief," he says, nodding to all of us before backing out of the room.

"Tina, you *know* you're supposed to take a bodyguard when you go off on your own," says my father, eyeing me sternly.

"When I think of what could have happened to you in this horrible city," my mother adds, still dabbing at her eyes with a lace handkerchief.

I roll my eyes at them, turning down the pink satin comforter and slipping into bed. "I'm sorry I worried you, but I'm fine. I'd just like to go back to sleep."

"I'm sure we all would," says my father, kissing my forehead before shepherding my mother out of the room and back to their suite.

"*Sei come una gatta*," says my brother, telling me I'm like a cat. "You have nine lives."

"*Meow*," I answer. "Turn off the light and shut the door, huh?"

"Someday you'll tell me how you snuck back in."

"Don't bet on it."

I grin at him, waggling my fingers in farewell as he pulls the double doors shut.

Taking a deep breath, I count to ten, just to make sure

that no one's coming back, then jump out of bed and knock twice on the hidden door that leads to the servant's hallway. A moment later, Ian steps into my room, pulling me into his strong arms.

"Aw, Tina," he murmurs, his heart thumping against my chest. "How'd you manage it?"

Without my heels on, I'm four inches shorter than I was before, which means my head nestles perfectly under his chin. "I made them think I'd been asleep in my dressing room the whole time."

He leans away from me, screwing up his face. "They bought that?"

"They did."

"That's the thing about the well-to-do," he says softly. "They never smell a rat."

"And if they did," I tell him pertly, "they wouldn't be rude enough to mention it."

We hold each other tightly, together again after the eternity of fifteen minutes apart, and I close my eyes, leaning my cheek against his chest as he kisses the top of my head with soft, sweet nuzzles.

As one second slides into the next, however, I become aware of the electricity between us: of how much I want him in ways forbidden to me, and how eager he would be to oblige me. My breathing becomes shallower and more ragged as I feel his fingers flex and tighten on my lower back.

"Now that you have me here, Yer Highness," he asks in

his low, gravelly voice, "whatever will you do with me?"

"Your *Serene* Highness," I correct him, suddenly feeling a little shy. Being felt up in a dark garden by a fellow royal doesn't quite compare with having an extremely male, undeniably sexy, Irish street thug visiting you in your hotel bedroom.

"What do you want, your *Serene* Highness?" he whispers.

"Everything," I answer, so softly I doubt he hears me.

"Come again?" he murmurs, lifting my chin so my eyes meet his.

"Kiss me."

He cups my jaw as he leans down, tilting his head at the last second so that his lips land flush over mine. We've kissed a dozen times tonight, but this time I'm only wearing a thin nightgown; the armor of my clothing is gone. I can feel the heat of his body through the flimsy fabric, but I am hungry for more. Trailing my fingers down his chest, I push at his t-shirt, grateful when he reaches behind his neck and pulls it off, leaving his skin bared to me.

My hands are flat against his chest when he unbuckles his belt and unbuttons his fly. I skim my fingers from his chest to his back, surprised when they slide still lower, and I feel the soft, rounded skin of his buttocks.

"You don't wear…underwear!" I say, leaning back and blinking at him.

He chuckles softly as he toes off his shoes and jeans. "Nope."

"You're naked," I add, uncertain of where to look.

"Uh-huh." He places his hands on his hips and grins at me. "Is that okay, princess?"

"Mm-hm," I hum, taking a step away from him so I can see him.

Moonlight—or impending dawn?—floods my room, bathing it in a soft, lavender light as I stare first at his face before dropping my eyes to his chest. In the luminous glow, I can make out a plethora of scars—some larger and discolored, others only ripples under my searching fingers. I land on one that's purple and the size of a five-cent coin.

"What's this?"

He covers my hand with his. "Stabbed."

"With a knife?"

"Screwdriver," he tells me.

My breath hitches as I look up at him. "Did it hurt?"

"It did," he answers softly.

I slide my hand from under his, tracing a jagged line under his left rib. "And this?"

"Glass," he tells me. "From a broken bottle."

My shoulders fall. "My God, Ian."

"It's nothin'," he tells me.

His hand covers mine, flattening it against his taut stomach before sliding it lower, until I feel curly, wiry hairs under my palm. I don't fight him. I don't protest. He holds his breath as my fingers touch the slick head of his erect penis, the pad of my middle finger circling the slippery crown.

By my hips, his fingers bunch in the fabric of my

nightgown. "Can I take this off?"

He is so much bigger than me. So much stronger. It makes tears spring to my eyes that he asks my permission for something that he could so easily take without it.

"*Sì*," I murmur, holding my arms up like a child as he tugs the cotton over my head and lets it fall to the floor in a whisper. My nipples tighten in the cool air, and I move instinctively closer to Ian. As my breasts skim his chest, he inhales sharply, cursing under his breath.

"Tina…Tina…Tina…" he groans, pulling my naked body flush against his. "I'll never recover from tonight, love."

Neither will I. I know it in my soul and in every beat of my heart. I care for this boy as I've never cared for anyone. After tonight, I will be changed. Forever.

"I want to…I want *us* to…" I murmur, grasping his arms and pulling him back with me until we fall onto the bed together, his broad chest covering mine.

"What do you want, love?" he asks, his hands tangling in my hair as his erection prods the delicate folds between my thighs.

"I want you to be…my first," I tell him in a rush, my cheeks flushing hot as a blush fans out over my whole body.

"Your…*first*? Wait, you've never…?"

I shake my head, swallowing over the lump in my throat. "Not yet."

"I can't believe you've never had the chance," he says, rolling to my side and searching my face.

"I have," I admit. "But technically, it's, um, *proibita*."

"Forbidden?" he translates. "Why? Because you're a princess?"

I nod. "Because my husband will expect to take my virginity."

"To...*take* it?" His forehead creases. "That sounds medieval. Is that what *you* want?"

"It's my duty," I tell him.

"Then maybe we shouldn't..."

"We should." I place my palm on his face, leaning up on my elbows to kiss him. "Some decisions in my life won't be mine, but this one *should* be." I kiss him again, lingering on his soft, full bottom lip until he groans. "I want this. I choose *you*, Ian Ladd."

"I choose you, too." He nods in agreement, his smile tender. "But it might hurt, *macushla*."

"*Macushla?*"

"It means 'my darlin','" he tells me, teasing my lips as I did his. "It might hurt, my darlin'."

Oh, my heart, this boy kills me dead.

"I know, *caro mio*," I say, pushing my body back until my head rests on the pillows. *But I want this.* I bend my knees and spread my legs in invitation, holding the pose rigidly. "Okay. I'm ready."

"Uh, well, h-hold on a second," he says, sliding up the comforter to kneel between my legs. He runs his palms up and down my thighs, and it's exciting and soothing at the same time. "We can...I mean, I can, uh, prepare you a little. Make it better for you."

My heart flutters like a trapped bird in a cage, beating so fast, it makes me dizzy. "Better?"

"Yeah," he whispers, leaning forward. "Better."

His lips slide slowly, gently along the soft skin of my inner thighs, his hair tickling my stomach as his fingers touch down gently between my legs. They spread me, exposing my core to the same cool air that puckered my breasts. Only a second later, however, the wet heat of his tongue warms me, my body flushing again as my hips lift off the bed.

He is tender and thorough, lovingly worshipping this secret place that's never been touched by another human being. I close my eyes and let my head loll from side to side, my breath hitching and shallow as he licks and laves, blows and sucks. A rising tide erupts in liquid heat within me, and I understand what he means about preparing me, because all I want amidst the quivering and shudders is to feel him inside of me. It's like he's unlocked a secret, primal gate that's simply been waiting for the right key.

"I want…y-you," I stammer, my voice breathy and thin as waves of pleasure make my sex tremble endlessly.

He slides up my chest, kissing me passionately with slick, salty lips, as his penis lines up at the entrance to my body.

"You're certain, *macushla?*" he asks me.

I force my eyes open, blinking at him as he hovers over me, his arms almost shaking from the self-control he's exerting.

"I am, *caro mio*," I breathe, rising slightly to welcome him as he slides into my body.

He is big and long, stretching my virgin tunnel until I cry out from the pressure, from the sudden stab of pain that makes me clench my muscles. But Ian has my permission, and with one final thrust of his hips, he impales me, his forehead meeting mine as puffs of hot breath land on my cheek.

"Are you okay?" he asks.

I can't lie to myself: it's uncomfortable and I will be sore tomorrow. But my heart floods with tenderness for this gentle man who has taken so lovingly what I offered, and who is trying to make the experience as good as possible for me. It's all that I could have asked for from my first time, and I will cherish the memory of being so intimately connected with one who—for one magical night—saw me for the girl I am instead of the princess I must be.

"*Sí*," I whisper, pressing my lips to his jaw. "Better than okay."

His hands are flat on either side of my head as he moves rhythmically in and out of my body, each stroke more comfortable than the last, the pain from my now-broken barrier receding with each kiss, each nuzzle, each intoxicated word of tenderness and praise.

My hands trail along the contours of his broad back, lightly, then harder, holding him tighter as his breathing gets faster, small grunts and groans of pleasure tickling my ear as he buries his head in my neck.

I know when he climaxes because he tightens everywhere and then relaxes with a deep, satisfied, "Ahhh" sound that makes my toes curl because it's me who's given him such pleasure.

He's heavy on top of me, but it's a blissful weight—hot and replete—and I miss it when he rolls to his side with soft pants, his eyes still closed, his lips turned up in a relaxed smile.

"Class," he sighs, chuckling softly as he turns to look at me. "Was that okay for you, princess?"

We both know I didn't orgasm with him, but how often does a virgin climax during her first time? I don't fault him for this. Not at all. And yes, the experience was good, most of all because I made the decision for myself, and because he made it as pleasurable for me as he could. Not to mention, I have feelings for him. *Real* feelings. Now that we've shared something so terribly intimate, I think it's possible that I love him.

"Better than okay," I say again, blinking my eyes against tears as I nestle into his side. "I will never forget it."

"It'll feel better next time," he promises, wrapping his arms around me as he yawns softly. "I promise, love."

"It was perfect," I tell him, closing my eyes as we drift off to sleep, and meaning it with all my heart.

CHAPTER 4

Ian

I told her I'd be back tonight.

And nothing but the end of the world could stop me from keeping my promise.

After we slept for an hour, we fucked again—slower and more tender the second time—and her little cries as we climaxed together were worth everything to me. I even murmured that I loved her. It was the first time I ever said those words aloud, and I meant them.

It would be impossible to spend time alone with Tina and not fall in love with her. Aside from her beauty, she's adventurous and fun, sassy and bold…and brave. *So brave*, I think, remembering her face as she gave herself to me, breaking the rules by which she's expected to live.

Her family's only in Limerick for one more night, but I'll be damned if we don't make the most of it. She's going to fake sick tonight and ask for dinner in her room.

And me? I'll gladly be courses one, two, and three.

The plan is for me to sneak in at seven and stay until dawn. It's twelve hours until then, more's the pity. But the streets of Limerick are quiet in the bright light of a summer morning, and I can't ever remember feeling this…happy.

I cross the River Shannon over Sarsfield Bridge, listening to the trickle of water and feeling the wind in my hair. The city's just waking up and there's a hop in my step as I pass by businesses starting to open for the day. I'm not certain I've ever noticed the flowers at Arthur's Quay Park before, jaunty and cheerful in the early morning sunshine. I might just pick a few for Her Serene Highness on my way back to her hotel tonight. Smiling as I consider bringing a token of love to a princess, I cross back over the river at Bridge Street, closer and closer to my neighborhood of St. Mary's Park. The house my grandparents left me mam, that I now share with Albie and Jarlath, is only a kilometer and a half from the princess's posh hotel.

But it's a whole different world here in St. Mary's Park.

Built as a local authority housing estate in the 1930s, it moved poor families out of the slums in the Lady's Lane and Parnell Street areas of the city and onto the northern end of King's Island, named, in part, for St. John's Castle, which is located on the southern end of the island, also called Englishtown.

Ain't much in common between those in St. Mary's and those in Englishtown, and if you're visiting Limerick, you'd be well advised to stay north of the Virgin Mary statue on St. Ita's unless you know what you're doing. This is Keegan-Clancy territory and no mistake. Them Murphy-Doyle bastards hunker down across the city, over in Ballinacurra Weston.

Fishing around in my pocket for the front door key, I'm surprised to hear voices coming from the kitchen. It's too early for Jarlath to be up and about on a Saturday morning, and Albie just makes himself an egg and watches the telly. But the voices I hear ain't on the telly. They're real. And raised in anger. It makes a chill go down my spine.

Making my way through the dingy front hallway, I step through a battered curtain into the kitchen where no less than seven men crowd the small room with Jarlath seated at the head of the table, half a bottle of whiskey in front of him.

"What happened?" I demand.

All eyes turn to me, but it's Sean, standing behind Jarlath, who flinches when he sees me.

Fuck me. Something bad's happened.

Jarlath looks up at me, his eyes bloodshot. "Ah, here he is. Finally home, eh? A little late now, boyo."

I don't look at my cousin. My eyes are locked with Sean's.

"What happened?" I ask again, my voice low and calm.

Men twice my age avert their eyes from me, looking down at the table, or out the grimy window over the sink. But not Sean. He stares straight back at me and I don't look away.

"Tell me," I demand, fisting my hands by my sides.

"It's Albie," says Sean, blinking like mad as he speaks my little brother's name. "I'm so sorry, Ian. He's dead."

He's...dead.

Albie's dead.

The room spins.

I can't breathe.

I reach for the counter to my left, lurching toward it, trying to steady myself.

Sean meets me there, and suddenly Luke's at my other side, arm under me shoulder, holding me up. My legs are jelly and I can't draw a clean breath because something awful is squeezing the life out of my lungs.

It's not the first time I've learned that someone has died.

But Albie.

Albie.

Fuck me and my miserable fucking existence, but I *never* thought it would be Albie.

"He…he was *twelve*," I bite out. "Twelve!"

My second cousin, Frank Keegan, stands up from his chair beside Jarlath, and Sean and Luke help me sit down. Swallowing back the lump in my throat and willing myself not to cry, I stare at the worn, wooden tabletop and ask:

"What *the fuck* happened?"

Sean and Luke flank me, with a hand on each of my shoulders, as Jarlath eyes me angrily.

"His older brother was off galivantin' with some Italian whore and weren't around to protect him!" spits my cousin.

"And where were you, ya gammy feckin' snake?"

His eyes narrow because we all know exactly where he was: here at this table with a full bottle of whiskey that's now half gone.

"It was Jack Murphy and his boys," says Luke softly. "Jumped him. Threw his bike in the river. Beat him bad."

AT FIRST *Sight*

"*Fuuuuck*," I hiss, my heart stuttering from the awfulness of it.

Why? I want to scream. *Why Albie?*

But I already know. Killing Albie was payback for what happened in the alley behind the theater last night.

"Don't think they meant to kill him," says Sean.

"What the fuck does that mean?" asks one of my Keegan cousins. "The lad's dead. Dead is dead. And they done it."

"Best we can tell, he was beat up bad, then hit by a truck whilst runnin' outta the park," Sean explains to me. "Blood all over his face, runnin' blindly, just tryin' to get away from those bastards…tryin' to get home."

"Where did it happen?"

"Park over on Oliver Plunkett. That's where he got hit."

The fields were originally designed for playing soccer and the like, but they've been used for seedier purposes over the last few decades. Albie and his mate, Colin Clancy, often meet there on their bikes to watch the goings-on.

"So Jack Murphy came into St. Mary's," I confirm.

"Yeah," says Luke. "Bold as fuck."

I slap my hands on the table. "Then we'll be payin' a visit to Ballinacurra Weston later today."

Sean lifts his hand, then resettles it on my shoulder. Luke does the same. They're in.

I raise my eyes to the older men at the table, a murderous rage racing through my veins. "I'll need a piece."

My uncle Brian nods. "I gotcha covered, Ian. It's old, but it works."

"I'll stop by at dusk," I say, knowing that we need to strike at night, in darkness, the same as they did to Albie. No doubt Jack Murphy will be at his favorite pub tonight, celebrating the death of my little brother. I'll get him right in front of his people, and I don't give a shite who knows or sees.

A plan for revenge settled, I fold my hands before me on the table. "Where is he? Albie?"

"Died at Bon Secours early this morning," says Luke. "They'll release him to family tomorrow."

"Wake on Tuesday," mutters Jarlath.

Bon Secours Hospital.

I passed it on my walk home this morning when I was dreaming about princesses and flowers; before my entire world came crumbling down around me. Little did I know then that my little brother lay cold inside.

No-show father. Crackhead mother. Mean, drunken shite of a cousin to look after us.

How were Albie and I supposed to survive?

We weren't. We never had a fucking chance.

I raise my eyes to my cousin who got us roped into the Keegan-Clancy gang wars in the first place.

With one furious swipe, I knock the half-finished bottle of Jarlath's whiskey off the table, listening to the glass shatter against the kitchen cabinets, littering the floor with shattered glass and spirits.

"This is yer fault," I tell my cousin, nailing him with my

eyes. "May ya rot in hell for it."

He puffs up his chest, like he's about to say something big, then suddenly deflates like a popped balloon, dissolving into sobs.

Because I can't bear another moment of this without doing the same, I push away from the table and walk away.

***

Sean and Luke are waiting for me in front of my uncle Brian's house at six o'clock.

I've spent most of the day in my room, crying and drinking, but I'm not pissed. I have a high tolerance for alcohol, and besides, nothing's going to keep me from getting revenge for Albie tonight. I've hurt plenty while brawling, but I've never killed a man. There's a first time for everything, and Jack-*fucking*-Murphy is going down. I don't care if I get a hundred years behind bars for the pleasure of watching him die by my hand.

My uncle teaches me the basics of how to use his Browning nine-millimeter handgun, warning me that the slide can sometimes jam.

"If that happens, hold the slide firmly in your weak hand," he tells me. "With the strong hand, strike the back of the grip. Repeat until the slide is freed, yeah?"

I nod, tucking the gun in the back of my jeans, and we're off to find Jack Murphy in his favorite watering hole, The Hollering Banshee, located near his Ballinacurra neighborhood. He won't be expecting me. Not this early. Not this soon. It's possible he doesn't even know that Albie is dead yet. For all I know, Jack and his boys didn't see Albie get hit. They could've split the second Albie ran off.

Plus, Jack's an overconfident fuck, I've learned over our weeks of rehearsals. Even if he knows Albie is dead, he'll think he's untouchable, being the son of Mary and Collum Murphy and on his home turf in Ballinacurra.

Fuck him and all Murphy scum.

They've got a rude awakening coming tonight.

As we take seats on the back of the 303 bus, I stare out the window, thinking about Albie's last moments—how scared he must have been to get cornered by the Murphys in a park considered safe for Keegans and Clancys. I wonder how he wiggled away from them and how far out of the park he had to run. The beating had to be bad if he had so much blood in his eyes that it blinded him from seeing the lorry headlights. Did he see it coming at him right before he got hit? Did he suffer? Did he cry out for Mam? Or for me?

My heart twists, and I clench my eyes tightly shut, opening them a few minutes later when we stop at a light…right beside the Limerick Palace Hotel. As the bus motor hums beneath my feet, I stare at the white marble building, briefly wondering if Tina's upstairs getting ready for me.

I won't be able to see her, of course.

I'll never see her again.

This morning, after I left her, as I was walking home, I thought to myself that it would take the end of the world for me to miss out on seeing her tonight.

Little did I know, my world had already ended.

***

"D'ya have him, Luke? Feckin' shite! He's slippin'! Hold him! Hold him upright!"

Sean is screaming and Luke is running, and I'm propped up between both of them as a searing, terrible pain shoots up my leg.

"Where t'fuck are we even goin', Sean? He's bleedin' everywhere. He's been bloody shot!"

I've been shot? I wonder, blinking my eyes. My heart is racing, but my breathing feels all wrong. Too slow. Too difficult. I can't draw breath. I can't think straight. My head is addled and thick.

"St. Anne's," says Sean to Luke. Then to me: "You'll be okay, Ian. Just a little farther."

"St. Anne's?" asks Luke. "The mental hospital?"

"It's close," pants Sean, "and besides, Trímian works there."

"Trímian, the director? Of the show? He's a bloody psychiatrist, Sean! We need a *real* doctor, for chrissakes!"

"Beggars can't be choosers," says Sean. "Ya holdin' up, Ian?"

Being half-dragged through the streets of Limerick with my leg on fire and my friends talking back and forth in short, terrified bursts doesn't have me feeling aces.

"Wha'…happened?" I mumble.

My voice doesn't sound right at all. It's soft and weak like I've been drugged.

"You shot Jack. Tavis-*feckin'*-Doyle shot you. We lit

outta there."

Sirens sound loudly in a neighborhood not too far away.

"When did I…pass out?"

"I dunno," says Luke. "It all happened so feckin' fast!"

I don't remember shooting Jack, and I don't remember being shot. The last thing I remember clearly was following Jack to the toilet. The rest is a blur of white-hot rage, shouting, and pain.

"Feckin' hell, Luke! Hold him up! I can't hold him alone. One more block."

I look up at the night sky, but I can't see the stars.

It doesn't matter.

I shot Jack Murphy.

My world goes black.

***

"Can you hear me, Ian?" A pause. "Ian, it's Dr. Trímian—er, uh, Eugene Trímian, the director of *Romeo and Juliet*. Can you hear me, son?"

I try to open my eyes, but the light is too bright. I clamp them shut quickly.

"That's it, son. Open your eyes."

"Where am I?" I rasp.

"Hospital," says Trímian. "St. Anne's."

"The mental hospital?"

"Day treatment center, yes. Can we try opening those eyes again, Ian?"

I open them slowly, wincing at the bright light, but managing to keep them open this time. "Can you…close the blinds?"

Trímian looks over his shoulder. "Oh. Sure. Yes."

Without the sunshine blaring into my eyes, it's easier to see. "Thanks."

"How about some water?" he asks, offering me a plastic cup with a straw.

I take a big sip, grateful for the cool water on my scratchy throat. "I was shot."

"You were indeed. Just above the ankle. Luckily, it didn't shatter the bone." Trímian pulls up a chair beside me. "Do you remember what happened?"

"We headed to the Banshee. Heads down. Saw Jack Murphy in the corner with his lads. He went for a piss. I followed him." And then…nothing.

"You bolted from the loo, out the door, and caught a bullet just above the ankle from Jack's cousin, Tavis."

"Is Jack dead?"

Trímian looks at me severely. "Do you want him to be dead?"

"Fuck, yes."

"You want to live with his death on your conscience for the rest of your life, Ian?"

"He killed my…" I can't say it.

"Your brother. Yes, I heard about what happened. I'm so sorry for your loss." Trímian clears his throat. "But killing Jack won't bring Albie back."

I lean my head back into the pillow, staring up at the ceiling as tears flow from the corners of my eyes. "How long've I been here?"

"Sean and Luke brought you in last night. You were lucky I was on duty. I had them bring you around back and we snuck you into an empty room on the first floor."

"That's me," I say. "So feckin' lucky."

"More than you know." Trímian reaches for my hand. "Jack Murphy *didn't* die, Ian. You got him in the shoulder. He's probably feeling about the same as you right now."

More useless tears join the ones already falling. And to my shame, half of them are because I'm so relieved to hear that I didn't kill pizza-faced Jack.

"I know," says Trímian, his voice soothing. "It's a strange mix of feelings."

"I wanted him to die," I insist. "To pay."

"His shoulder'll bother him for the rest of his life. He won't be able to forget what happened to Albie whenever it aches, and that's better punishment than dying."

There's comfort in his words, and I cling to it.

"We need to talk." The doctor squeezes my hand. "You've got to leave Ireland, son. A dozen people saw you follow Murphy into the jacks and come out with a smoking gun. You'll go to prison for sure."

"And feckin' Jack what killed Albie?" I demand. "Will he be in the cell next to mine?"

"Albie's death is being ruled a traffic accident. Only one other child—a friend of your brother's—can testify that Albie was beat up by Jack Murphy, while Jack has relatives all over the city that will swear he was nowhere near St. Mary's on the night Albie died."

"Fuck!" I scream, throwing my cup of water across the room. No justice for my brother. Jail for me. "And Tavis?"

"Claimed self-defense. He was in the neighboring toilet stall when you shot Jack. Gave him a valid reason to shoot at you." Trímian pauses here, letting go of my hand. "The only one in real trouble here, Ian, is you."

"They know I'm here?" I ask.

Trímian shakes his head. "No, lad. I wouldn't rat you out."

"Why not?"

"Why do you think I started the theater program in the first place?" He cocks his head to the side and when he speaks again, his accent is heavy and streetwise like mine. "Me mam was a Clancy."

"You were…part of it?" I ask, meaning that the good doctor was part of the ongoing gang wars between the four families.

"Could've been," he says, his posh voice back. He shakes his head. "But, no. I had an aunt in Killarney who took me in young. Got away from it. Went to school, became a doctor…"

I nod. "You escaped."

"I was given a chance, thank Christ," he says, running a hand through his gray hair. "And I'd like to do the same for you."

"Well, I don't have a rich auntie in the country," I snipe.

"Tell me this," says Trímian, his green eyes searching

mine. "If you could make three wishes, son, what would they be?"

"Life ain't a fairytale," I inform him.

"Answer me anyway."

I blink at him, my eyes filling with more fucking tears. "To have my brother back."

Trímian winces, placing his hand on my shoulder and squeezing. "I'm a decent doctor, son, but I can't bring people back from the dead."

"Feckin' lot of good you are," I tell him, snot dripping from my nose. I sniffle pathetically, lifting my arm to wipe it away and then on the crisp white sheet that covers my chest.

"You need a fresh start, lad," says the doc. "You must have people somewhere. In Boston? New York?"

I shake my head. "The only people I know are here."

Which means I'll be arrested for attempted murder, tried as an adult and put in jail before my seventeenth birthday. I sniffle again, hating the weakness of crying, but Lord Jesus, I guess I have a right to a few tears what with losing Albie and being shot and all.

Trímian takes a deep breath. "I watched you, you know, while you were in the play, during rehearsals."

"You a poof, doc?" I ask him, leaning away from his touch.

"I'm not," he says, chuckling softly as he removes his hand from my shoulder. "Married to Jenny Trímian twenty-six years and counting."

"Why'd you watch me special, then?"

"You're a good kid, Ian. A born leader. You were the

first to offer a hand to the Murphy-Doyle kids and your boys followed your lead. There's potential in you." He puts on his "street" voice again. "But you gotta get the feck outta Limerick, son."

"I got nowhere to go," I say softly.

"What if you wished for a passport, a plane ticket and a place to stay?" he suggests.

"Sure. And while you're at it, a million quid, doc."

"You're on your own to make the million, but I've got a sister in Brooklyn. You know where that is?"

I shake my head.

"It's right near New York City. Just a bridge away."

New York City. I've always dreamed of it, of course, but never dared to believe I'd actually get there. My life is in Limerick. Always has been. Always will be.

"So what?" I ask him.

"Her name's Brenda and my brother-in-law's Craig. Good people. They own a pub." He chuckles softly. "An Irish pub called Prince's Tavern. Nothing special here, but the locals there love it."

"Good for them."

"They never had kids, Ian. I think…" He frowns for a moment, then sighs. "I think Brenda and Craig'd welcome the chance to help out a good kid who's had a rough time."

"Would they, now?"

Trímian nods. "I think—no, I *know* they would."

I want to believe him. So badly it actually hurts. But I'm suspicious too.

"Nothing's free," I say. "What would I have to do in return?"

His expression straightens, and I can see the street kid he may have been thirty or forty years ago, because he's ice cold when he says, "Never come back. And never, ever speak of what happened."

I stare at him, amazed by the change in him. His eyes meet mine and it's impossible to look away because Eugene Trímian, local doctor and amateur theater director, is terrifying when he channels his Clancy side.

"I mean it. I won't be an accessory to what happened last night. I won't go down for aiding and abetting. I patched you up, and I'll help you leave, but I never want to see you again, Ian. You can never speak of *me* or of *what I did* to help you. Not a word. Ever. Do you understand?"

The stakes are high for Dr. Trímian—he's putting his neck on the block to help me, and I will never betray him by putting him in danger.

"I swear it on my Keegan heart," I tell him solemnly, offering my hand.

"That's good enough for a Clancy," he answers, shaking it.

PART II:

Shear Heaven

(Three Years Ago)

Dear reader:

So sorry for the interruption! But, at this point, if you haven't, I'd advise you to go ahead and read:

Shear Heaven is the love story of Valentina's brother, Nico; it takes place three years ago, in New York City, during Valentina's wedding to shipping magnate, Steve Trainor.

You don't have to read *Shear Heaven*, of course, and **you will still be able to understand and enjoy the remainder of *At First Sight* even if you skip *Shear Heaven*.** But

Valentina figures prominently in Nico's story, where the circumstances of her marriage to Steve Trainor are briefly discussed and explained.

Whenever you are ready, read on!

Xoxo

PART III:

Present Day

CHAPTER 5

Present Day

<u>Valentina</u>

"Mamma!"

My three-year-old daughter, Carina, sitting in a sea of half-packed moving boxes, lifts her arms for me and I pick her up, nuzzling her soft cheek against mine.

"*Che cosa, bambina?*" *What's up, honey?*

"I want *Babbo*," she tells me solemnly, brown eyes searching mine.

"*Babbo* went to the angels," I tell her for the hundredth time. "I miss him too."

"The angels needed him?"

"Mm-hm. They needed a good man like *Babbo*."

"And he'll never come home again?"

Of all the difficult emotions I've experienced since Steve's sudden passing, trying to explain his loss to our daughter, Carina, has been the most excruciating. Steve and I didn't have a typical marriage, but we became very good friends during our three years as husband and wife. I loved him very much and missing his friendship and company is a constant ache.

"No, *bambina mia*," I tell her, resting my lips on her

forehead. "But he'll always love you. *Babbo* is your angel now. Forever."

She nods, but her eyes are sad. *Too* sad for a three-year-old child.

We desperately need a fresh start, my daughter and I, which is precisely why we're moving out of the mansion we shared with Steve in Genoa, and into the loft apartment he owned in Brooklyn, New York.

Of all the properties around the world once owned by my husband, and now by me, this one is the closest both to Steve's place of birth and to the church in Manhattan where we were married. I think that's why I chose it. Because a marriage I dreaded at first and only half-tolerated for the first six months, evolved into the most loving and stable friendship I have ever known.

"Will *Babbo*, the angel, know where to find me?" asks Carina, cupping my face with her chubby, little hands. "Even if we move away from here?"

"*Sí, vita mia.* He'll *always* know where to find you. I promise."

With that, she sighs softly, offering me a little smile before wiggling out of my arms and running out of the house, into the garden. I cross my arms over my chest as I watch her go, wondering if I'm making the right decision for us. But when I look around the home we three made together, I know that staying in Genoa isn't possible.

For the record, my husband, Steve Trainor, a successful international businessman and billionaire, was also homosexual.

We married each other because we needed to: I was a pregnant, unmarried princess, whose family was in debt, and he was a billionaire, plagued by rumors about his sexuality that had always bothered him. By wedding one another, my daughter, Carina, was legitimized, my family was given a generous allowance, and whispers about Steve's sexuality became non-existent. We lived quite happily in and out of the public eye until three months ago when Steve, who loved steak, eggs and rich sauces almost as much as he loved Carina and me, died suddenly and instantly of a heart attack.

He wouldn't have felt any pain, the doctors assured me, and I was grateful. But in the face of losing my best friend, partner and the only father my daughter had ever known, it was cold comfort.

I miss him.

Some days, I miss him so much—his cheerful smile and wonderfully warm bear hugs—that I cry myself to sleep. Never, not for a single day in my entire life, had I ever received the level of unconditional acceptance, kindness and safety that Steve offered me throughout our three happy years together. He was a good man. The best.

And the reality is that other than my twin brother, Nico, my life hasn't been full of good men. If anything, manipulators, users and abusers always seem to gravitate to me instead.

"Highness?"

I look to the entrance of the dining room where my bodyguard, Gaspare, stands with his hands on his hips.

When I married Steve, Gaspare and Iago joined us in Genoa, heading up the security team that Steve already had in place.

But since Steve's death, something about Gaspare feels different. I can't put my finger on the exact change because it's very subtle; but I notice his gaze lingering on me sometimes, and for the first time in my whole life, his presence makes me slightly uncomfortable.

That said, he is familiar to me, and I still trust him. *We are all probably adjusting to Steve's loss and our upcoming move to the United States*, I tell myself. I'm sure that's all it is.

"*Buon giorno*, Gaspare," I say, my once-stilted English now filled with colloquialisms learned from my American husband. "What's up?"

"The packers have finished lunch, madame. They'd like to come back inside and resume their work."

"*Va bene*," I tell him, looking around at the chaos. We leave for Brooklyn in four days, yet so much still needs to be packed away in storage or shipped overseas to meet us. "What would I do without you?"

"You'll never need to find out," he assures me, his homely face searching mine in a way that makes me feel slightly uncomfortable.

"Thank you. I'm grateful to you and Iago for agreeing to come to Brooklyn with us."

"We would not trust New York with Italy's greatest treasure," he tells me solemnly.

"I don't know a soul there," I say. "At least I'll have you two with me."

"I wish to be always by your side, princess."

"You're an excellent employee," I answer, reminding him of his place. "Tell the movers they're welcome to come back inside. I'll be with Carina in the garden if I'm needed."

"Yes, madame," he answers, giving orders into the com on his watch.

Picking up my husband's laptop from the kitchen counter, I make my way through one set of double doors that leads to a vast, sun-soaked, stone patio that looks out over my daughter's "playground." That's what Steve called it, but it's more of a one-person amusement park village if you ask me. A lifelike little town built with child-sized buildings and fully furnished for an active three-year-old, he spared no expense in making it the perfect place for imaginary play. I grin as I watch her "shop" at the market with a little cart custom made for her with her favorite doll in the front basket.

"How is she, Iago?"

Once my brother's loyal bodyguard, Iago is devoted to my daughter now. Nico and Bella live in Lugano, near Lake Cuomo, and employ a minimal staff at their penthouse, choosing to live as commoners instead of royalty. They had no need for Iago's services, so I gratefully accepted him into my employ.

"She is a survivor," he tells me. "She misses Signore Steve, but she is strong…like her mother."

"I'm going to relax for a bit," I tell him, gesturing to the pool area. "If she asks for me, you'll know where to find me."

"Of course, madame."

Once I'm settled on a lounge chair in the sun, I open Steve's computer to a file called "If Anything Ever Happens To Me" and look through the many documents and spreadsheets Steve saved there, overwhelmed by his thoughtfulness all over again. He made sure that I would have a step-by-step instruction manual for how to deal with his holdings in the event of his passing, and though I'd never wish him gone, I am so grateful for his instruction and advice from the grave.

I have already sold many of his homes, only keeping this house in Genoa, an apartment in Lugano near my brother, another apartment in London that I love, and the $8M loft in Brooklyn where he grew up. If I decide I want to purchase more property in the future, it won't be a problem. I have inherited most of Steve's billions.

He told me to keep my seat on the board of his largest company, Trainor Shipping, and urged me to place everything else under the discretion of Trainor Capital Management which will send me quarterly checks for my profit shares of Steve's many businesses. Carina and I will be looked after for the rest of our lives, which makes tears of gratitude spring to my eyes.

The rest of my life.

But what the hell am I going to do with it?

In the "If Anything Ever Happens To Me" file, there's a letter saved as "Personal Advice for Valentina," which I open and read again for the twentieth time.

My darling and most cherished friend,

You are only reading this if I am gone, and if I am gone, please let me tell you that the years I spent as your husband and Carina's father were the richest and best I ever knew. Thank you for giving this gay, old bachelor the chance to parent such a marvelous little girl and care for her beautiful mother.

He goes on to talk about the many bounties of our marriage, which he calls "the most fun he ever had," and tells me to show Carina the pictures and videos one day: of her fabulously popular mom and dad—at movie premieres and state dinners—who tricked everyone in the world into believing their epic love story.

Maybe it wasn't so far from the truth, though. Like you, I had many nameless, faceless lovers, Valentina, but you and Carina, in your own ways, were the true loves of my life.

That said, and because I promised never to bullshit you...I need to say something important and I want you to hear me, my stubborn darling.

Though you always said you told me everything, I believe there is one part of your story that you withheld even from me: I believe you loved someone once as passionately and romantically as one human being can love another. He left you or hurt you or betrayed you, or all three, and from that pain, all of your ideas about sex and love evolved. You neither trusted nor sought true love in your life. You only gave your heart to me because you knew I couldn't break it.

A brief montage of unwanted memories suddenly flicker behind my eyes:

A black curl that won't be tamed.

A jagged scar on a muscled chest.

I love you, macushla. I love you.

My facial muscles tighten in a wince and my eyes narrow as an expelled breath through my nose—a short, furious puff of air—returns my thoughts to here and now. I blink at the screen, forcing those images away and finishing Steve's letter to me.

Whoever he was, you must find him and face him and bid him farewell forever. Until you do, I fear he may always haunt you, keeping your heart in a cage of your own making, and standing in the way of the sort of deep and lasting happiness you deserve.

Be well, my darling friend, my beloved wife.
Kiss the bambina.
And know how terribly I loved you both.
Your Steve

As tears flood my eyes, I push the laptop closed and stare at the still water of the aqua blue pool, wondering what new life awaits me in Brooklyn.

***

Ian

Every year on August sixteenth, I take an hour to sit on a very particular bench at the Brooklyn Botanic Gardens.

It's one of many ordinary-looking benches—with stone legs and wooden slats—but it bears a bronze plaque on the back which reads: *Albert Dylan Ladd. Beloved brother. Never forgotten.*

It's Albie's memorial, and the place I feel closest to him in my adopted country.

The bench cost $25,000 when I purchased it for the gardens—it took all of my savings and a loan from Craig that took three years to work off. These days I could buy a hundred such benches without blinking an eye, but I wouldn't remember the sweat I'd broken in the making of each and every dollar. It's the memories of my little brother, combined with that hard work, sweat and tears, and that binds us together here, on these worn and weathered wooden slats.

"Daddy!" cries Dylan, racing over to me with an acorn. "It has a cap!"

I grin at my son: at the ray of sunshine who's my favorite person on earth. "Yes, it does. Who taught you that?"

"Miss Meyer," he tells me, referring to his pre-school teacher.

I know Miss Meyer. I know Miss Meyer very, very well, right down to the light brown mole on the inside of her upper left thigh.

"How about you find me five more just like it, huh?" He scrambles off to do my bidding, my four-year-old horticulturist who loves these gardens just as much as I do.

It was in these gardens, in fact, that I met Brenda Prince for the first time, fifteen years ago. Dr. Trímian had instructed me to take a cab from Kennedy Airport to the Brooklyn Botanic Gardens where his sister Brenda worked as a groundskeeper. She met me at the front gate with a warm, welcoming hug, commenting on the orthopedic boot that kept my injured foot stabilized.

"Good thing I brought a golf cart," she'd said. "Hop in beside me. I'd like to show you something."

Throwing my small bag on the back seat, I sat down beside her, and we were off, the warm, summer breeze blowing in my hair as we made our way into the park. She pointed out various plantings and gardens as we rode along, her soft Irish burr watered down with an American accent she'd no doubt adopted during her years in New York.

"Here we are!" she'd finally declared, stopping the cart by a sign that read: Cranford Rose Garden.

And even me, a gang kid from Limerick, couldn't be stoic at the threshold of such abundant fucking beauty. Roses of every color bloomed like a rainbow, their faces angled to the sun. And the smell? I'll never forget the smell for as long as I live. It smelled like heaven. It reminded me of Valentina De'Medici, the princess I'd loved so passionately for one unforgettable night.

"Every year," said Brenda, still seated beside me, "this rose garden has what we call, 'A Second Flush,' when it enjoys a replay of its June glory for a few weeks at the end of August. It's a second chance to see the roses in full bloom." She turned to me and tilted her head to the side. "A second chance, Ian. That's what Gene wanted for you. That's exactly what you've got here with us."

Brenda wasn't subtle, but she was kind, and I understood her meaning. I could muck up the gift that she, Craig, and Dr. Trímian had offered in setting me up in America, or I could lean into it and make something of myself.

With nothing to lose, I decided on the latter.

I started working with Craig at Prince's Tavern the week I arrived: washing out glasses, mopping the floor, restocking the salt and pepper shakers, bussing the tables—whatever he asked of me. For the first time in my life, there was a hot meal on the table every night, courtesy of Brenda, and no, she wasn't the best cook I ever met, but I wolfed down everything she ever made and told her I loved it because I was grateful.

After a few months, Brenda and Craig hired a private tutor to get me up to scratch for the GED, a high school equivalency test given every spring in the states. I aced it, but only because my teacher, Ms. Donegan, was a regular harpy, on my case all the time; and because I wouldn't let down Brenda and Craig for all the tea in China. They believed in me. I couldn't—I *wouldn't*—reward that trust with failure.

With my high school diploma under my belt, I applied to take classes at CUNY-Brooklyn, grateful when Craig flipped my work schedule so it wouldn't interfere with my class load. And when I graduated from college four years later with a bachelor's degree in business, Brenda and Craig sat in the second row, clapping for me like proud parents.

They have been better parents to me than anyone could ask for, and my loyalty to them—and to Dr. Trímian—is absolute. Families are formed when you're born, sure, but they're also formed when people take you in and love you for you. Not because you can do something for them, but because they're so fucking kind and decent that they give you a second chance to prove that you're not trash to be thrown away; that given that rare and precious second chance, you might even make something great of it.

That's Brenda and Craig: my family. My fairy godparents on earth, and no mistake.

Fifteen years later, I'm staring at the same rose garden in the same month, and the roses that greeted me in America so long ago are the same that my son plays amongst now. His dark hair, midnight black in the sunshine, is easy to spot as he zigs and zags through the many rows of roses.

I love him more than I've a right to love anyone.

He's only the second person, in the whole of my life, to whom I've actually said the words, "I love you," and meant it.

And the other?

"It was perfect, Caro Mio."

My white angel.

Princess…

The other is more and more like a dream as the years roll by.

"I found three more!" Dylan calls to me.

I grin at him, holding up my hand, finger splayed. "I said *five* more, boyo!"

He gets back to work, little flip flops smacking against his feet as he scampers around the garden.

For the record, I didn't love his mother.

We dated for a handful of months five years ago, on-again, off-again, on-again, and finally off-again when she dropped off Dylan at my apartment and told me he was mine and she was going back to France. Red-faced and furious, strapped into a car carrier, he looked so much like me, I didn't doubt it, though I still did a DNA test once the shock had worn away. Because Dalia had no interest in being a mother to our child, the courts gave me full custody when he was six months old, and it's been him and me ever since.

Well, actually—

"Grammy! Grammy! The acorns are falling early!" he exclaims to Brenda, who's found us in the roses.

—him and me, *and* Brenda and Craig, who love him like he's their own.

She bends down to his level, holding out her hand. "Show me, then, lad."

Is her accent stronger when she's speaking to Dylan or is it just me? I wonder, grinning at the pair of them.

"Daddy wants six and I only got four," he complains.

"Well, how about Grammy gives you a hand, then?"

He pulls Brenda to another oak tree as she looks over at Albie's bench and waves to me. I wave back, gratitude filling my heart. *I'd be nothing without them*, I think. They softened my edges and opened my heart. Brenda believed in me, Craig trusted me, and Dylan thinks the sun rises and falls in my eyes.

For the record, I made good on my second chance.

I own nine "Prince's Tavern" pubs in Brooklyn, Staten Island, and Westchester County, New York, now, and I brought Brenda and Craig along for the ride, setting them up for life with the payouts from their initial investment.

I also own the latest model Jaguar, wear a Rolex on my wrist and bought myself a posh duplex in Williamsburg, not far from where Brenda and Craig still live in Bay Ridge. My kid doesn't want for anything: he has a room of his own with every toy on the market, his favorite foods in our cupboards, top-notch babysitters who come with the highest ratings, classes at the local Botanic Garden, a father who loves him and two doting grandparents.

I've done well and it's a sweet life…but for one thing:

I have no one special to share it with, the lovely Miss Meyer notwithstanding.

And yeah, she's eager enough to spread her legs at the end of the night, but there's no…magic. No magnetism. Nothing special. We eat dinner, we chit-chat, we drink wine, we fuck, and I promise to call her again sometime.

And I do…eventually. But we're friends-with-benefits more than anything else.

The truth is, I've had many lovers in my life, both before knowing Valentina and after, but I've never known her equal. When I told her I'd never recover from that night, truer words were never spoken. I never did.

I also knew there wasn't a chance in hell she'd ever forgive me for standing her up that night. I can only imagine what she thought of me as the minutes ticked by and I didn't show. It's what kept me from reaching out to her all those many years.

And then, about three years ago, a tabloid picture caught my eye as I was ducking into the Foodtown on my block. Lo and behold, there she was in all of her serene glory; a picture of my Tina with the caption: *HSH Princess Valentina Yasmina De'Medici, in Manhattan for her marriage to shipping magnate, Steve Trainor.*

I picked up the newspaper and stared at her picture for several minutes, my held breath depleting as I drank in the sight of her again after so long. Her light blonde hair, swan neck and pouty lips were the same. She wore a diamond tiara, poufy white wedding gown and string of pearls around her neck as she stood beside her new husband on the steps of St. Patrick's Cathedral.

My white angel.

But it was her eyes that captivated me, that haunted me hours later when Dylan was asleep in his crib and I made my way through a bottle of Irish whiskey. They seemed…flat. Empty. Unhappy. It felt like a dagger to the heart, the lack of sparkle and mischief in those once dark and dreamy eyes.

I looked up Steve Trainor on the internet, and from the rumors swirling around him, I gathered that her marriage might not have been a love match. And I wondered, just for a moment, if that was my fault—if Tina had had to marry someone who didn't care about her virginity because she didn't have it to give.

It still bothers me, that picture of the sad princess I'd loved for a few short hours on one magical evening so long ago.

But my life is here now, years and distance away from the streets of Limerick where I was a stupid, fucked-up kid, and she was the once-in-a-lifetime girl of my dreams.

"Daddy!" yells Dylan, racing toward me with Brenda at his heels. "We have six! Me 'n Grammy did it! We found six!"

I grin and lean forward, ready to clasp him in my arms the moment he reaches me.

CHAPTER 6

<u>Valentina</u>

"Mrs. Trainor?"

"Yes. This is she."

"I'm calling from the Brooklyn Botanic Gardens. This is Carina's teacher. Miss Meyer."

"Oh!" I put down the cup of tea I've been nursing, my brows furrowing. "Is something wrong?"

"Um…well…no. The *short* answer is no. Carina is safe and sound."

With a sigh of relief I ask: "What's the *long* answer?"

She pauses for a moment. "Would you be able to stay after for a few minutes at pick-up? I'd like to chat with you."

"Is there a problem?"

"Not of Carina's making," she says. "But we had some tears today. She's being bothered by another child, and I'd like to speak with you and the other child's parent after pick-up. If you're available."

"Of course," I tell her. "I'll…I'll be there at noon and plan to linger."

"Wonderful," says Miss Meyer. "And again, this is really nothing to worry about. We deal with these sorts of situations all the time and believe strongly in bringing in parents to help us resolve these situations with the children."

"I understand," I say, nodding as I look through the living room picture window at the knock-out view of Manhattan. "See you soon."

"Thank you, Mrs. Trainor. Goodbye."

Hmm. I wonder what's going on.

Carina hasn't seemed upset or dragged her feet about going to school.

Could the young, overly perky American teacher with nice skin and no style be overreacting? Children quarrel, don't they? Nico and I certainly did.

Sighing with annoyance—about the meeting and the bullying—I pick up my teacup, sipping slowly.

I have heard the horror stories about royals and celebrities treating their children like breakable crystal, and requiring that everyone in their children's orbit do the same, but I refuse to raise Carina like that. As much as possible, I want her to have a normal childhood. I won't shelter her from the ups and downs of life. There are disappointments. There are sometimes bullies. None of us are exempt from challenges and it's best we learn that lesson early.

That said, however, Carina is so young, so little. Her English is good from being Steve's daughter, but she's new to America, new to Brooklyn. She arrived here a few weeks ago with one parent, her heart still heavy with grief. Why does this other child have to pick on her?

I frown, placing my teacup on the glass coffee table in front of me.

The sofa I'm sitting on was made in Italy—the white leather is supple, but the cushions are still stiff. I suppose it'll take some time before everything feels…lived in. That said, after a month of unpacking and redecorating, the elegant tenth-floor loft in the building where Steve grew up has become a home for Carina and me. Moreover, Brooklyn itself has become a haven for us. Like many other celebrities who choose to live out of the Manhattan limelight, I love the quick access to Manhattan, but prefer the cool, artsy, down-to-earth vibe of this neighboring borough.

We have met quite a lot of families in our upscale building—likely because there's a gorgeous rooftop garden and play area on the twelfth floor where we sometimes commune in the evenings, swapping tips about pre-schools and watching our little ones burn off steam.

It was there, in fact, where I learned about the Brooklyn Botanic Pre-School program and hastened to enroll Carina in their September session. Full disclosure? The class was full. But mentioning my status as an Italian royal (*and an eager donor*) helped the powers-that-be find one extra spot. So my daughter, growing up in such an urban environment, now attends classes every weekday at the local garden. For me, it's a perfect balance. I thought it was for her, too.

I glance at the time.

It's eleven o'clock already, and I still need to shower and dress before my meeting with Miss Meyer and this other child's mother.

May it be mercifully brief, I pray, so that Carina and I can have some lunch al fresco at the Yellow Magnolia Café before naptime.

***

It was my sister-in-law, Bella, who suggested we check out the Brooklyn Botanic Gardens as soon as we were settled into our new home, and I will be forever grateful to her for the suggestion.

It is here that I feel most comfortable, most soothed and from whence I always leave refreshed.

Gaspare and I take a cab, as we do on the days I pick up Carina instead of Iago, to the Eastern Parkway entrance, flashing my membership card as I pass through the gates. It's a fair walk to the Children's Botanic Garden, but I ask Gaspare for some privacy on the half-mile summer stroll. I'd like to do some thinking. The sun is high, but there's a late-summer breeze. I pass by the Cranford Rose Garden, detouring through the Japanese Hill-and-Pond Garden, which is Carina's favorite spot with its charming bridges and jaunty red torii.

I wonder why another child is bullying her, and though I try to tamp down my protective instincts, they rise up unexpectedly with each step forward. I remind myself that bullying is a part of life and that all challenges must be met head-on, but the conviction I felt in my apartment dilutes. For whatever reason, I imagine this other child with two parents, living happily in Brooklyn, not having to deal with the heartache of a recently deceased father.

How dare she bully Carina, who has been through so much?

"*Calmati*," I tell myself, as I speed walk past the café

where we often have lunch, but it's easier said than done.

Why am I paying to have my daughter here in this place, where she is being abused by other children?

My temper is flaring, but before I meet this other mother, I need to get it under control. It won't do to arrive flustered and furious.

I slow down at the Water Garden, reminding myself that the other child is just as small and young as mine, still learning important life lessons about how to treat others. My anger has no place in the meeting I'm about to attend.

Trying to distract myself, I check out my reflection in the pond—Gucci sunglasses, butter-yellow silk tank top by Escada, cropped Lily Pulitzer jeans in white, and chic Valentino wedges—and raise my chin.

You are a princess. You can be disapproving without being terrifying.

And then I turn to the right and continue on to the Children's Garden.

"Wait for me here?" I direct Gaspare, who nods, stationing himself nearby.

Surrounded by a cream-colored picket fence, the Children's Garden is where Carina is dropped off and picked up every day; it's also there that she tends her own garden plot, plays games with the other children, has a mid-morning snack at the picnic tables and does seasonal art projects with materials collected from the many surrounding gardens. Per usual, the children are outside playing when I arrive, Carina and another little girl staring down at something on the ground while Miss Meyer explains that caterpillars turn into butterflies. She looks up as I approach, shielding her eyes.

"Mrs. Trainor. Hello."

"I don't want to interrupt you," I tell her.

"Not at all," she says, standing up. "I was just telling Carina and Millie about Mr. Caterpillar."

My daughter looks up at me before springing to her feet and wrapping her arms around my legs. "Mamma!"

"Hello, darling."

"Miss Meyer said I get to stay extra today."

"That's true," I say, sliding my eyes to Miss Meyer. "Is Millie's mother here yet?"

"Oh!" she says. "No. It's not Millie who..." She looks over at a group of boys sword fighting with twigs. "Dylan! Can you come and join us?"

A little boy with dark hair and blue eyes turns from the pack to look at her, his expression curious and defiant at once. "Do I have to?"

"Yes, you do," says Miss Meyer, her voice even and kind. "Come along now. I want to speak to you and Carina inside."

His shoulders deflate as an annoyed expression passes over his features, and though I stifle it, I want to smile. Something inside of me admires his spirit.

"Ooo-kay," he sighs, walking over to us with lead feet. "But my grammy's not here yet."

"Actually," says Miss Meyer, a slight blush pinkening her cheeks, "your *father* is coming to join us." She glances at her watch, then looks up, a winsome smile exploding across her features. "Look! Here he is now."

I turn my head, following her gaze to the tall, dark-haired man stepping inside the picket gate. He wears a business suit and sunglasses, but there's something instantly familiar about him and a shiver trails up my arm, even though I'm standing in a beam of August sun.

As he approaches, he pushes his sunglasses to the top of his head, revealing dark blue eyes fringed with long, dark lashes. My heart quickens to a double-time beat as my eyes glide to his left cheek, daring the scar *not* to be there.

But it is.

It is.

My God, it's *him*—HIM!—developed from the film of my dreams.

"Sorry I'm late," he says, coming to a stop in front of Miss Meyer. "Traffic."

Even after fifteen years, I recognize the low grittiness of his voice, the soft burr of his brogue rolling the *tr-* sound. Without realizing it, I hold the breath in my lungs as he slides his eyes to my face.

With a shaking hand, I reach for my glasses, pulling them from my eyes and listening as my breath releases raggedly.

"Ian," I whisper.

His eyes widen, then narrow, the rest of his face slack with shock as he leans closer, scanning my features.

"Tina?"

I nod, too dazed to follow-up with any comment of meaning. He is older. Taller. Broader. He is a man now, and when he left me all those years ago, he was still a boy.

But I recognize him. I see him. I see the boy I knew in the man before me.

It's him! my heart sings.

It's him, my mind spits.

"You already know each other?" asks Miss Meyer. "Oh! That's terrific. Then, this should be quick." She gestures to the education building. "Shall we go inside and chat for a few minutes?"

Ian's eyes trail across my face, lingering on my lips before quickly seizing my eyes again. We stare at each other, unmoving except for our chests, which rise and fall with similar shallow breaths.

"Mamma?" asks Carina, who is still standing against my legs. "Miss Meyer wants to go inside."

"Y-Yes!" I blurt out, finally turning away from Ian to give Miss Meyer a deranged smile. "Of course. *Andiamo*."

I let Carina pull me inside.

***

Ian

When Dylan's nanny, Angela, who generally picks him up at school, told me that Miss Meyer had called about him bullying another child in the class, I insisted that she not call Brenda and told her that I would attend the parent-teacher meeting myself.

I don't believe in handing off dirty work to someone else. If Dylan is being aggressive or mean-spirited, it's up to me to tackle the problem with him and make appropriate apologies and promises to the parent of the other child. It's called 'responsible parenting,' and it's important to me.

That said, I assumed I'd meet with the kids, Miss Meyer and some young, hip Brooklyn mom. Dylan would say he was sorry. I would promise to work on better behavior at home. And then, if Brenda would come and collect Dylan for lunch, I might even be able to fit in a quickie with Rachel—ah-hem, Miss Meyer.

Never, ever—not in my hottest, hungriest, or wildest dreams—did I imagine the mother of the bullied child would be Valentina De'Medici. If anyone had warned me, I would have called them daft. I couldn't have fantasized such a meeting. I wouldn't have allowed myself such a bittersweet delusion.

And yet, here I am, following her, our two children, and their teacher into the education center at the Brooklyn bloody Botanic Gardens. My mind skims seamlessly over the years to the last time I saw Tina. She was dulcet and naked, her gorgeous body only half covered by tousled sheets, and she'd offered me a dreamy smile as I waved farewell and slipped out of her hotel room through the secret door.

How I wanted to stay.

How I wished I could have offered her the world.

How the entire course of my life changed that day.

She is as beautiful as ever and a quick glance at her ass in tight, white jeans confirms that her figure hasn't suffered from motherhood. She's gorgeous. My one-time dream girl has blossomed into a vibrant, stunning woman.

"Take a seat," says Rachel, gesturing to a ridiculously low table with six tiny chairs. "This will only take a minute."

The kids sit down side by side, and Rachel sits beside Valentina's daughter, presumably in solidarity of the wronged party. Valentina sits next to Rachel, and I take a seat beside my son, feeling ludicrous on a chair so tiny, my knees almost touch my chin.

When I look up, I zero in on the fact that Rachel and Valentina are sitting side by side.

And call me a bastard, but I'm sorry to say that Rachel, who's been a decent friend-with-benefits, suffers in comparison. She's young and fresh-faced in her yellow t-shirt and denim overalls—but no more than a kid herself, really, with none of Valentina's life experience or gravitas.

In contrast, more a princess now than she ever was, Her Serene Highness radiates composure, sophistication and grace. I have a quick flashback to standing on that stage in Limerick, the first night I ever saw her—how struck I was with a desperate, concentrated urge to *see* her, to *know* her, to *touch* her, to *be* with her.

All over again and without warning, those feelings flood my being for the second time in my life as she raises her eyes to mine, then quickly looks away.

"So!" says Rachel, looking back and forth between me and Valentina. "How do you two know each other?"

Valentina's dark eyes flick up, glancing at me first, then Rachel. "We met years ago. In Ireland."

"Oh, my goodness!" says Rachel, looking at me with a

too-big smile and questioning eyes. "So you're old...*friends!*"

"Sort of," I say at the same time Valentina says, "Not at all."

Rachel chuckles awkwardly, speaking into her fist like it's a microphone. "Ref, can we have a verdict?"

"It was a very brief meeting," Valentina says dismissively.

"We haven't seen each other in—" I start to say.

"Fifteen years," finishes Valentina, her eyes flashing with anger for a second before she lifts her chin and offers Rachel a cool half-smile. "We're here to speak about the children, right? Perhaps we should…"

Rachel nods emphatically. "Of course. Business before pleasure!"

I stare at Valentina as Rachel asks the kids to tell us about the incident at snack time, but I can't concentrate on what's being said.

Tina is pissed. Even after fifteen years, she's furious with me.

I clench my teeth, tightening my jaw as I look down at the colorful, paint-stained tabletop.

Of course she's furious. She trusted me with her virginity, and once I took it, I abandoned her. She has every right to be angry.

But may I confess that there's another part of me—a visceral part that exists in my most basic id self—that's fiercely and intensely turned on by her anger? The very nature of fury is passion. And mine is skyrocketing in response to hers.

"...and was that a kind thing to say, Dylan?" Rachel asks my son in a stern voice.

Dylan wiggles in his seat, his little knee brushing against my massive one and snapping me back to reality. I take a deep breath, telling myself to calm down.

Don't look at Valentina again. Not until this meeting is over.

"Sorry," I say. "Can we back up? Start over?"

Rachel cocks her head to the side, her expression vaguely disapproving, like she'd like to rap my knuckles (or bum) for not paying attention. Though we've actually role-played at teacher-student once or twice, I'm not even a little bit aroused by the notion. If anything, it just makes me feel uncomfortable now.

What was I thinking dating someone over ten years my junior, just out of teacher's college? I need to break things off with Rachel. The sooner, the better.

"I'll recap," says Rachel. "At snack time today, Dylan intercepted Carina at the trash bin, about to throw out her apple slices. Apparently, he told her that children all over the world go to sleep hungry, and if she didn't finish her snack, she'd go to Hell."

"Dylan said that?" I demand, shifting my eyes to my son, who's looking down at the table miserably. "Son, did you say that?"

"Sure, I did," he tells me with a bit of shaky bravado. "Father Darren says that at CCD."

"That yer goin' to *Hell*?" I cry, my accent stronger because some gobshite priest has had the gall to tell a four-year-old he's going to Hell!

"He said that wasteful children are naughty, and God has a special place for naughty children," Dylan explains, all bravado disappearing as tears gather in his eyes. "And he means *Hell!* I don't wanna go to Hell, Daddy! I don't want Carina to go either!"

Damn it, I knew that Brenda and Craig's church was too old-school for Dylan's and my sensibilities. I should've followed my instincts, but they made it so easy, picking him up every Sunday morning for services and every Thursday afternoon for Catholic education.

Well, no more. I'll find somewhere else for us to attend mass more in line with our modern views and values.

I pull Dylan onto my lap, my heart squeezing when he buries his face in my neck and cries. Rubbing his back, I whisper, "It'll be alright, lad. You won't be goin' back there again anytime soon. I'm sorry, son. I'm sorry Father Darren frightened you. You're far too good for Hell. The second they saw you comin', they'd chase you back up to Heaven."

When I look up, Rachel's watching me with Dylan, a distinct look in her eyes telling me her eggs are ready to meet my swimmers. Lord, I'm going to need to break off our affair gently.

Valentina, on the other hand, is far more reserved. She observes us, her face betraying nothing that she may or may not be feeling.

"Carina," she finally says, taking her daughter's hands. "You are not going to Hell, *bambina*. Not now. Not ever. And not for throwing away apple slices. It's...*assurdo.*"

"But Dylan said—"

"Dylan has been frightened by an adult who is a—a jackass," she says, reaching for her purse. "We can discuss it more over lunch, *vita mia*." Glancing at Miss Meyer, she asks, "Is this all? Can we go now?"

"Oh, well, usually we have the children shake hands and—"

"Dylan is upset, and Carina is hungry," she says, her voice no-nonsense as she stands up from her chair and pulls Carina up with her. "They can shake hands tomorrow, okay? Yes?"

Dylan's sobs have subsided now, and he looks up at me with bleary eyes. "I'm hungry, too. Can we go to lunch with Carina and her mom?"

"You know," says Miss Meyer, "I think that would be an excellent idea. It would be therapeutic for the children to share a meal, and—"

"My treat," I say at the same time Valentina says, "No."

But Carina has other ideas. "I *like* Dylan! And we're *not* going to Hell anymore. I want to have lunch with him. *Per favore, Mamma?*"

Valentina looks at me, her eyes cool. "I'm sure Dylan and his father have other plans, *bambina*."

She wants me to give her an out, but I can't. I won't. I need more time.

"No, we don't," I say quickly. "Have lunch with us. Please. We can go to the Yellow Magnolia. It's just down the—"

She takes a deep breath and huffs. "We know where it is."

"Please, Mamma!" says Carina. "Lunch date! Lunch date!"

"Lunch date! Lunch date!" joins Dylan, scrambling off my lap to jump up and down next to Carina.

I raise my eyebrows at my one-time love. "Lunch date?"

She crosses her arms over her chest, her expression extremely annoyed, but then she looks at the kids and sighs.

"*Va bene*," she says softly. "Lunch date."

***

The kids race ahead down the path that connects the Children's Garden to the nearby café, so Valentina and I are left to stroll together, side by side, with her bodyguard following behind like a chaperone.

We're quiet for the first few minutes, and I wonder if she, like me, is thinking about that magical night so many years ago when we raced around Limerick and ended the night in each other's arms.

"It was a shock," I finally comment, "to see you after so long."

"Hmm," she hums. "Yes."

"How long have you lived here? In Brooklyn?"

"My husband passed away several months ago. We moved here for a…" She clears her throat and sighs as though the next words don't apply anymore. "…fresh start."

"I remember reading somewhere that you'd gotten married," I tell her. "I'm sorry your husband passed away."

This is a lie. On a caveman level, I'm not sorry at all. No. Scratch that. To be clear, I'm sorry if she suffered in losing him, but I'm not sorry that she's single.

"Thanks."

"Where were you living before?"

"Genoa."

"What made you choose Brooklyn?"

"Steve," she says. "My husband grew up here. I guess…I just wanted to feel close to him."

There is a well of emotion behind her words that lights a spark of jealousy within me. Could the rumors have been untrue? Was Steve Trainor heterosexual? And was Valentina the love of his life? Was he hers?

I have no right to feel hurt by this or jealous or it, but fuck it—I am.

I can't help it.

"You must miss him," I say.

"I do," she answers. "Very much."

"And you?" she asks. "How did *you* end up here?"

How I want to tell her everything: that the night I was with her, my brother was killed. And the night I was supposed to meet her, I was shot. And that two days later, I was on a plane bound for New York City.

"Uh. Relatives took me in," I say, giving her the same shallow, detail-less backstory I give everyone. "Heard about the street violence in Limerick and uh, invited me here. Gave me a fresh start, um…soon after—I mean, not long after that night. When we first—"

"Yes," she stops me, her voice curt.

The kids stand in front of the cafe, waving to us from the glass doors.

"We're here," she says.

I put my hand on her arm, and it knocks the breath from my lungs when she stops walking and raises her eyes to mine. They're hurt and angry, her lips a thin slash of pink in her otherwise stunning face. I've dreamed of it a million times. How strange and wonderful to behold it before me once again.

I will win you back, Princess. I swear it.

"I'm sorry," I whisper, fifteen years of regret packed into two meager words.

She blinks at me before pulling her arm away.

"I don't care," she says, stepping forward to push open the cafe doors and following the kids to an available table.

CHAPTER 7

<u>Valentina</u>

I'm sorry.

I'm sorry.

There are a million and one ways to say the words "I'm sorry," and I can't stop thinking about the way Ian said them to me yesterday in front of the café. So full of regret, he was practically choking on it, the words were soft and tender.

If he hadn't stood me up fifteen years ago without a word, I might have even believed them.

But he *did* stand me up, I recall, tears stinging my eyes even after all these years. And after what I'd given him, after what we'd shared, it was so painful, there are some days I still don't know how I survived it.

For weeks after leaving Ireland, I was despondent. Spending hours on my own, crying in bed or peeing near-constantly—and saying rosaries to the Virgin for my period to arrive—I was alone in my grief and fear. I brutalized myself for my stupidity in believing he loved me. I hated that I'd trusted him. I was crushed that something that had felt so real was just a pile of steaming shit.

And even after my period arrived, ensuring that our tryst hadn't led to an unwanted teen pregnancy, the emotional repercussions from that night reverberated through my adolescent life, affecting my views on love and sex for…ever.

I could never again trust my instincts or intuition about men, so I didn't try to make a lasting emotional connection with them.

If my body felt like fucking, I found someone to fuck me. Sex was just sex—a physical act that led to physical pleasure. Nothing more. Nothing less.

If my heart felt like falling in love, I doubled-down on my conviction that love couldn't be trusted. I'd fallen in love once at fifteen and been played for a fool. I wasn't eager to repeat the experience, no matter how much I longed for a meaningful connection with someone.

Sitting on my stiff, white couch with my morning cup of tea, and desperately needing some comfort, I open the "Personal Advice for Valentina" file on Steve's laptop. As I read his letter again, I marvel at how well he knew me. A fresh wave of grief makes tears slide down my cheeks and blur the words I know by heart:

I believe you loved someone once as passionately and romantically as one human being can love another. He left you or hurt you or betrayed you, or all three, and from that pain, all of your ideas about sex and love evolved. You neither trusted nor sought true love in your life. You only gave your heart to me because you knew I couldn't break it.

It should be impossible that a fifteen-year-old princess and sixteen-year-old street thug should, in one night, form a connection so profound that they are haunted by it for years, and damaged by it for life. But the unlikeliness of it doesn't make it less true or more deniable.

It happened then.

It happened yesterday.

I felt it all over again when our eyes met in the Children's Garden: in the electric-like currents of energy that zinged and zapped between us. In the shock and awe that I suffered in *my* heart and read on *his* face.

But then, Ian and I never lacked chemistry. We had it in spades.

I have learned a great deal about chemistry in the years since I knew him. I'm an expert on the topic, and I know better than anyone that even the greatest chemistry doesn't equal love.

I loved him passionately and romantically.

He left me, hurt me and betrayed me.

And I neither trusted nor sought true love again.

Steve was right. On all points, he was right.

However unbelievable it might seem, I loved Ian. I gave my body to Ian. And Ian used me, then walked away.

Whoever he was, you must find him and face him and bid him farewell forever. Until you do, I fear he may always haunt you, keeping your heart in a cage of your own making, and standing in the way of the sort of deep and lasting happiness you deserve.

I close the laptop, sipping my tea and looking at the view of Manhattan. It's gray today; a hazy cityscape through storm clouds and drizzle.

Find him and face him? Check.

And bid him farewell forever.

Even as I nod my head, my heart drops.

Bid him farewell.

Forever.

I bite my bottom lip, thinking about our lunch date yesterday.

I wish I could say that he was boorish and unpleasant, but he wasn't. He was a perfect gentleman and a wonderful conversationalist. While the children colored their menus and giggled at inside jokes, he gave me a quick update on his life: moving to the states soon after our meeting in Limerick, staying with kind relatives who'd given him a job and helped him through school. He owned a solid business now—several flourishing American restaurants that emulated typical Irish pubs—and a condo not far from me in Williamsburg. When I asked about his wife, he explained that he'd never been married to Dylan's mother and she was no longer in the picture. My heart held its breath as he answered and sighed with relief to learn he was single. Poor, stupid heart, more vulnerable than ever to this man, my living, breathing kryptonite.

Bid him farewell forever.

I know I should.

I have his business card. I should ask to meet him for a drink and use the opportunity to tell him goodbye. Sure, it will be awkward, but it would be for the best, wouldn't it? It would be an exercise in self-care, in resolution, in closure. It would be me, taking back the reins of my life after fifteen years, and finally freeing my heart from a "cage of my own making."

Gaspare enters the living room and clears his throat.

Our bodyguards share a suite of rooms on the west side of the loft that includes two small bedrooms, a sitting room, kitchen, and bathroom.

"*Buon giorno*, Gaspare."

"*Buon giorno*, madame. Shall I have Iago pick up *la bambina* today?"

"Yes, please," I tell him with a grateful smile.

"And we're taking you to a museum this afternoon?"

I nod. "The Guggenheim in Manhattan. There's a parent-child class at three on watercolor painting."

"Very well, madame."

He stands in the doorway for a long moment, as though he has more to say. *"Che cosa, Gaspare?"*

"Mr. Prince, madame," he says, his expression souring at the mention of Ian's name. "The man you met yesterday at the gardens."

"Yes," I say.

"I've done a bit of digging."

"You don't need to," I tell him. "Mr. Prince and I have met before."

"Is that right?" he asks, his eyes narrowing.

"Yes. I should have mentioned it yesterday, but I was distracted…"

"Because we can't find any background on him. He appears, fully formed, in Brooklyn, about fifteen years ago."

I nod. "As I said, I know him. You don't need to waste

your time looking into him. He's…nobody."

"I see, madame." He hesitates for a moment before adding, "Still, if you'll be seeing him, even occasionally, I feel strongly that we should—"

"Cessare, Gaspare!" I exclaim, then take a deep breath, reminding myself that Gaspare is only interested in my safety. "You do not need to look into him. I'm telling you not to. Do you understand?"

I have no interest in Gaspare and Iago learning about my ill-fated fling so many years ago. My cheeks heat at the very notion of being discovered. Ian was my secret. I want him to stay that way.

"Very well, madame," says Gaspare, his voice clipped and hurt. "As always, I act only for your safety."

"Of course," I say. "I'm sorry for snapping at you."

He nods his head in deference, then turns to leave the room without another word.

Coming to Brooklyn was supposed to mean a fresh start for Carina and me, not a deep dredge of past hurts. Not only do I want to hide my teenage shame from Gaspare and Iago, I want to hide it from everyone. I have no interest in revisiting it, only bidding it farewell.

Hurrying to the front foyer, I fish Ian's business card from my purse, and before I lose my nerve, I dial the number on the front.

My heart races as his phone rings.

Beep beep. Beep beep. Beep—

"Hello?"

"Ian, it's Valentina."

I can hear his breath exhale in a sigh, and my toes curl.

"Valentina. Hello! Yes." He laughs softly. "I'm so glad you called."

Chemistry, I tell myself. *It's only chemistry and history. Nothing real. Nothing more.*

"I thought we should maybe meet," I tell him.

"Yeah. That'd be grand. Do you have a sitter yet? I could take you to dinner."

"I have staff to watch Carina," I tell him. Telling him that I have no interest in knowing him and asking him to keep his distance from me and my daughter won't take more than half an hour. "But there's no need for dinner. I think a drink would be better."

"Sure," he says. *Is that disappointment in his tone?* "A drink. Okay."

"Can you suggest a place?" I ask, cradling the phone against my shoulder and rubbing my sweaty palms on my leggings.

"How about one of mine?"

I long to see what he's made of himself, but if I did, every time I passed one of his restaurants, I'd think of him. *Best keep this impersonal, Valentina.*

"Just somewhere in Williamsburg," I say. "Nothing special."

"Right," he says slowly. "Nothin' special. Huh. Okay. How about Juliette's?"

"Is that a joke?" I ask, remembering the play I saw on the night we met.

"No."

"Are you trying to be cute?"

"I'm not takin' the piss, Tina. I promise. It's a French spot in Williamsburg. On North Fifth Street."

Cagare, I'm nervous.

"Okay. Fine. Juliette's. I'll meet you there."

"When were you thinkin'?"

"Tomorrow night."

"Eight o'clock?"

"*Va bene*," I whisper. "See you then."

Before he can say anything else, I hang up.

The sooner I see him, the sooner I can say farewell. The sooner I say farewell, the sooner I can move on and find the "deep and lasting happiness" my dear Steve wished for me.

Dio Mio, may it be so.

***

Ian

Thank the Lord my sitter was free tonight because there's no way I was going to miss out on the chance to see Tina.

If I'd had no other choice, I would've taken Dylan to Prince's and left him behind the bar with Craig for an hour or two. It's not an option I like to exercise, but the lunch we shared two days ago wasn't nearly enough time with her.

Since reconnecting, I can't think straight. I can't think of anything but explaining to her, as best I can and without betraying my promise to Dr. Trímian, what happened that night in Limerick. She deserves to know that the situation was fucking extenuating. A real and sincere tragedy was the *only* thing that could have kept me from returning to her.

In the hopes of seeing her again, I picked up Dylan twice more this week, disappointed when Tina's bodyguard arrived to pick up Carina. That extra time at school did, however, give me a chance to talk to Rachel. As gently as possible, I told her that I'd met someone, and though I hoped we could remain friends, there wouldn't be any more "benefits" to that friendship.

Although she seemed surprised, she regrouped quickly, telling me that she was seeing someone from her art class, and if we were over, she'd pursue something more serious with him.

More's the better.

From the moment I saw Valentina again, I haven't been able to think of another woman, nor quell the fierce longings of my heart. Those old feelings—that should have died a thousand deaths by now—have returned tenfold. But this go 'round, I'm not Ian Ladd: a teenaged street rat without a dollar to my name. I'm Ian Prince: a successful businessman. This time, I could—if she'd let me—romance her proper.

Fucking let me, Princess, I think to myself as I walk to Juliette's. *See me. Consider me. Give me another chance to prove that fate brought us together and the gods don't make mistakes.*

I push open the door and walk into the Parisian-style café, complete with hanging plants that droop lazily from suspended pots. Hanging lanterns splash soft light onto bistro tables and a ceiling of glass lets a little moonlight shine through. This is my favorite restaurant in Brooklyn, and if I'm going to bare my soul to a princess, it may as well be here.

"Ian!" says Jacqueline, one of the hosts who knows me. "Waiting for someone or solo tonight?"

I kiss her cheeks. "Waiting for someone."

"Lucky someone," she says with a giggle. "You want a table?"

"We're just having drinks."

"Ah. Well, do you want to wait down here or on the roof? I can send her up when she gets here."

Rain lashed the city yesterday, but it's clear and warm tonight. The rooftop sounds like heaven.

"You don't mind bringing her up?"

She shakes her head. "Not at all. What does she look like?"

Ah, Lord. How to describe Her Serene Highness Valentina Yasmina De'Medici to someone who's never seen her before…

"Um, well. She's not tall. She's thin…w-willowy-like. She's got this, like, very blonde hair…" I chuckle softly. "First time I ever saw her, it looked like a halo, you know? She looked like a bloody angel. And, uh, well, she's got dark eyes. Very dark. And stormy when she's mad. She's…" I look up to see Valentina stepping into the café, and my heart thrums like I'm sixteen all over again. "… here."

Jacqueline, whose face has softened while I've been speaking, turns around, "*Bienvenue, mademoiselle.*"

"*Bonsoir. Merci beaucoup,*" says my princess in perfect

French, bestowing a demure smile on the hostess.

"Hello, Tina," I say, leaning forward to kiss her cheeks in greeting, but she pulls away, putting her hand between us. Slightly embarrassed, I draw back, taking her hand and shaking it. "Good to see you."

"*Bonsoir*, Ian," she says, dropping my hand quickly.

"To the roof," says Jacqueline, grabbing two menus. "Follow me."

I gesture for Valentina to precede me and she does, following the hostess up the stairs. She's wearing a little sundress tonight. It's blue and white tie-dye, and ends just above her knees. Though I've never been, it reminds me of pictures I've seen of Greece—of the bright blue sky and crisp, white-painted buildings. Her legs are tan and her hair, in a braid that ends at the base of her neck, is platinum blonde.

Other parts of her are that color blonde, too, I remember, and it makes my heart skip a beat.

"Will this table do?" asks Jacqueline, leading us to a quiet spot in the corner of the rooftop garden.

"Yes, thank you," says Valentina, letting me pull out her chair. She sits down, then offers our host a small smile. "Can you bring some sparkling water, please?"

"I'll tell your waiter. Anything else?" she asks, looking back and forth between us.

"A martini," says Valentina.

"Scotch on the rocks," I add, sitting down across from her.

"Of course," says Jacqueline. "*Bon apetit!*"

I watch as Valentina settles her small purse on the table to her left, then takes her napkin and spreads it in her lap. She is unsmiling, and seems troubled, and suddenly, I have misgivings about why she invited me here.

"Thank you for meeting me," she says, raising her eyes to mine.

"I'd meet you anywhere, anytime," I tell her.

Her face changes, going icy in a split second. "We both know that's not true."

"Tina—"

The waiter returns with a bottle of sparkling water and pours us each a glass. "Your drinks will be here soon. Would you like to order an appetizer?"

"No, thank you," she says softly, her voice firm.

"Very good. I'll be back in a minute," he says, stepping away.

Valentina clears her throat and starts her speech over again. "Thank you for meeting me. I have a favor to ask."

"Anything."

"Carina and I have come to Brooklyn for a fresh start. Losing Steve was very hard on both of us, and I had hoped this would be a safe place to build a new future. With that in mind, I'd like to ask you not to—"

"I couldn't come back that night!" I blurt out. "It wasn't possible."

"Excuse me?"

"I—I couldn't come back to your hotel room like I promised—that night in Limerick. I wasn't—I mean, I *would have*, I *wanted to*…but I *couldn't*. It was impossible."

She blinks at me, then purses her lips.

I can tell there's a battle going on behind those dark and stormy eyes. I'm fairly certain she was about to tell me to fuck off and leave her alone when she started her speech, but now she's curious about what happened that night.

"What do you mean?"

"That morning. I told you I'd be back that night—"

"You told me a lot of things," she snaps.

"I meant them, Tina! It was the best night of my life. Not just up to then. Up to *now*, love."

She raises her eyebrows, then reaches for her water and takes a sip. Two spots of pink have appeared on her tan cheeks, and they betray the emotion she's feeling. They give me hope.

"Then it shouldn't have been impossible," she says softly.

"My brother died," I say, the words tumbling from my mouth. "While we were together that night in your hotel room, he died."

Her lips drop open in horror as she raises a hand and flattens it over her heart. "What?"

"He was hit by a truck," I tell her, wincing at the memory of walking into my kitchen on that terrible morning. "He was…killed instantly. I passed Bon Secours Hospital walking home from your hotel. Had no idea Albie was lying in the morgue."

"Oh, Ian," she whispers, her eyes filling with tears. "I

didn't—how awful. I'm so very sorry."

"You didn't know."

I place my hands on the table, palms up, hoping that she'll—

Yessss.

I sigh with pleasure when she covers my hands with hers, the touch of her skin against mine making my breath catch and heart soar.

"You thought I stood you up."

She nods, sniffling softly. "I did. I thought…terrible things."

"About me?"

"And about me," she says, still nodding. "What an idiot I had been to trust you."

"Your trust wasn't misplaced," I tell her. "It was just bad luck."

The waiter returns with our drinks and she pulls her hands away to dab at her eyes with a napkin.

"Only a tragedy could have kept me from seeing you again," I assure her.

The two spots on her cheeks grow pinker and her breasts rise and fall more rapidly with her breathing, which is shallow and quick, like mine.

"I wish you'd gotten word to me."

I gulp. *How much can I tell her in good conscience?*

"I couldn't," I tell her.

"Why not?" She blinks at me, then looks down at the table. "No. Forget I asked that. I'm sorry. Your brother had just died. You'd only known me for a few hours."

"No! I—I wish I'd been able to get word to you, but I...I didn't handle it well. Albie's death. I ended up in hospital. By the time I was clear-headed, you'd left Ireland."

"The hospital?" Her brow furrows. "What happened? Were you injured somehow?"

Now it's my turn to look away. If I say much more, I'll betray those who helped me, who saved me from prison. And I don't have the Princes' permission to do that. "He was my only sibling. I drank. I acted rashly. It was a dark time."

"I understand," she says. "I'm so sorry, Ian. Losing your brother must have been...terrible."

"It was. But it was a long time ago," I say, finally taking a sip of my own drink. The fiery liquid burns my throat, but every sip after the first will be smoother. "Hey...were you going to tell me to leave you alone? When we sat down? It felt like maybe you were headed in that direction."

She takes a deep breath, then sighs. "Yes. That's why I asked to meet you."

"Does knowing why I didn't come to you that night make a difference?"

"It solves an old mystery," she says, still keeping her feelings close.

"I'm sorry if I hurt you," I tell her.

She shrugs. "Like you said, bad luck."

That sounds too much like a segue into goodbyes for my taste, and I have no interest in saying farewell so soon.

"Hey...don't you think it's strange that we've met again

by chance across an ocean? Both single. Both with one child. Maybe the universe is trying to tell us something."

"The universe?" she scoffs. "I'm not sure I trust the universe."

"Then trust *me*," I plead with her, leaning forward in my seat and desperately trying to find the words that might give us a second chance. "If Albie hadn't died, I would've come back. Who knows? We might even still know each other."

"That's not likely, Ian, is it?"

No, it's not, I guess. But it doesn't matter. I want another chance. I need to convince her to give me one.

"Maybe not. But *possible*."

She takes a sip of her drink.

"Tina, listen…I think…I think my heart's been asleep for fifteen years. I didn't know it. I didn't realize it until I—until I saw you again. Until I—quite literally—felt it wake up on Tuesday morning. If you walk away from me now, I'm afraid it'll go back to sleep, and never wake up ever again."

It's a more flowery speech than I'm used to, but I'm willing to do whatever it takes to not be jettisoned from her life. And besides, it's true. It's all true. Seeing her again has awakened something within—something that I only felt once before in my life: the night I met her.

She bites her bottom lip. There's so much fear in her dark eyes when she levels them to mine, but I'm heartened when she nods for me to continue.

"You trusted me that night, right?" When she doesn't answer, I narrow my eyes. "You said you did, at the time."

"I guess I did," she murmurs.

"Then, give me another chance, *macushla*," I ask her, my voice low and gritty with emotion. "Now that I've found you again, don't ask me to stay away. Please."

It feels like an eternity that I sit there waiting for her response. So long, in fact, I'm about to slide onto the floor and beg her from my knees when she says:

"Come for dinner on Saturday. You and Dylan."

Am I hearing her right? "Wait. What?"

"Dinner. Saturday." Her lips wobble like she wants to smile, but won't quite let herself.

That's okay. I'll smile enough for the both of us. I'm fucking shocked and terribly pleased by her unexpected invitation.

"You mean it?" A little chuckle of joy escapes from the back of my throat, surprising me. "Dinner? At your place?"

"Yes," she says, her tiny smile dimming. "But don't get your hopes up. I don't really trust *anyone*, Ian. I'm not good at it."

"I just want to get to know you again," I tell her. "We'll take it slow…and, I won't let you down. I promise."

"We'll see," she whispers, her eyes cautious. Then suddenly, out of nowhere, that tiny smile reappears with a little shrug of her shoulders. "Everyone has to eat, right?"

"Right," I say, my heart swelling with so much hope, I'm surprised my chest can hold it. Whoever would have guessed that the sweetest words ever are these: "Everyone has to eat."

CHAPTER 8

<u>Valentina</u>

Our second date as a family is even smoother than the first, with the children playing together in Carina's play room while my Chef makes us dinner, which leaves Ian and me alone to enjoy a glass of wine in the living room.

"This was your husband's apartment?" asks Ian, standing by the window in a charcoal gray suit. He is tall and beautiful, staring out at the dusky skyline of Manhattan.

"Yes," I tell him. "I renovated and decorated a bit, of course, but yes, this was Steve's childhood home."

"I read about him," says Ian, glancing at me. "He was a brilliant businessman."

"He was a brilliant *person*," I tell him, taking a sip of the chianti he brought as a gift. It's a surprisingly excellent bottle and reminds me of home. "I loved him very much."

Ian's posture changes just a little at this admission—stiffening a touch—and it occurs to me that, like the rest of the world, he is probably under the impression that Steve and I were a love-match.

"How did you meet?" he asks, his voice low and soft.

"Blindly," I admit. "A week before our wedding."

His neck snaps to the right, his eyes boring into mine.

"What?"

I exhale softly. This isn't a truth I've told many people outside of my family and very close friends, but I can't seem to help myself. Whether it's the smartest or stupidest thing I've ever done, I'm not sure. I only know that since learning of the tragic and terrible reason he stood me up so many years ago, I want to trust Ian.

"Ours was an arranged marriage," I say softly. "The rumors about Steve's sexuality were true."

"He was…homosexual," Ian confirms, staring deeply into my eyes.

I nod, taking another sip of wine, and looking back out at the view. "He was."

"Then why…?"

"He wanted a wife to allay rumors about his sexuality, and I needed a husband. I was pregnant with Carina…and unmarried."

"Unacceptable for a young royal," mutters Ian, no doubt remembering what I told him that night in Limerick so long ago.

"A Catholic one, anyway," I say. "I could've ended the pregnancy, I guess, but I didn't want to. I wanted to be a mother. I wanted her."

"Did you love Carina's father?" he asks in a low voice.

"Honestly?" My cheeks flush hot. I wonder if he'll judge me harshly for what I'm about to share. "I'm not sure who he was."

"Oh."

"I've had many lovers," I confess boldly, lifting my chin. He may as well know the whole truth. "None of them meant anything to me."

"Except one?" he whispers, leveling me with those dark blue eyes.

I nod, my own eyes burning, because he's right and we both know it. "Except one."

You.

Me.

He takes a sip of wine, then murmurs: "I see."

Does he? Does he understand that losing my virginity to a young man who—by all appearances—seemed *not* to value it, taught me not to value myself? Taught me that my body was something to be shared at random, without commitment or expectation?

When Ian lowers his glass and turns to me, his eyes are so sad, I feel his compassion in my heart, in my gut, everywhere.

"I see you, Tina," he says again, answering my questions. "I *see* you. And you are as beautiful as you ever were. As lovely. As funny. As smart. As perfect."

"I'm not," I say, leaving him at the windows and taking a seat on the white couch.

I made my choices, and the truth is that most days I don't regret them. I'm not ashamed that I like sex. I sowed my wild oats and slept around, and yes, I got pregnant out of wedlock, but from that phase of my life came my greatest treasure: Carina.

I wouldn't trade some of it, for fear that I'd lose it all.

He follows me, placing his glass on the coffee table, and taking my hand in one of his. With the other, he reaches up to cup my cheek gently, tenderly.

"Believe me, love, because I was *there*, and I am *here*, and I *know*. You are every bit as magnificent now as you were then."

My eyes close slowly and I lean my cheek against his hand, mewling softly at the warmth of his touch. I haven't been touched by an available, heterosexual man in over three years, and I've missed it. Add to the equation that the man touching my face was the only man to *ever* touch my heart on any meaningful level, and it's almost enough to make me swoon.

"Mamma! Mamma!"

"Daddy!"

The sound of racing feet makes my eyes open and I leap to my feet, as though afraid of being caught doing something naughty by a chaperone.

"Darlings!" I say, smiling at dark-haired Dylan and bright-eyed Carina. "*Che cosa?*"

"What does *that* mean?" asks Dylan, hopping on his father's lap.

"It means...*What's up?*" I tell him.

"In what language?"

"*Italiano!*" announces Carina, who stands beside Ian, looking at his face intently. "Are you Italian like me and Mamma or American like *Babbo*?"

"I'm not either," says Ian, with a grin that makes my

heart flutter. "I'm Irish."

"What's that?"

"Irish? Means I'm from Ireland." He chuckles. "It's a little island in Europe, off the coast of England."

"I been to England," Carina informs him.

"Have you, now?"

"Yep," she says. "It's the place with the Ferris wheel."

"London."

"Yep. London," confirms my daughter. "It's fun there. Me and *Babbo* went on it lots. Mamma was a'scared of heights so she waved at us from the ground."

"Why don't we go to London?" asks Dylan. "How come Carina gets to go?"

"I took you to Disney World," says Ian.

"Yeah...but, if we're Irish, why we never been to Ireland either?" demands Dylan.

If I wasn't watching so closely, I would've missed the way Ian's grin faded. "Because we live here."

"Dylan! You gotta see the upstairs playground!" exclaims Carina. "Mamma, can Iago take us?"

I glance to the foyer where Iago sits at the ready on a chair by the front door. "Of course. You don't mind, Iago?"

"My pleasure, princess," he says, standing up.

"Have them back in twenty minutes for dinner?"

"Of course," he says, with a deferential nod.

Alone again, I sit down next to Ian on the couch, picking up my wine glass and taking another sip. "They're cute together, aren't they?"

"He told me he loves her," says Ian, smiling at me. "I

don't think he was bullying her last week. I think he was trying to protect her, actually."

"From Hell?"

"I'd do the same for you," says Ian, his voice rumbly and low. "Brave it to rescue you. Take your place if I had to. Anything to keep you safe and whole."

My breath catches and I have a sudden and intense flashback to his bloodied knuckles after he fought off those boys in a Limerick alley.

"That boy," I say, trying to remember his name. "The one from the alley. Um…Jack. Jack Murphy, right? Whatever happened to him?"

Ian's face, which was so tender and warm a moment ago, freezes. He stands up, leaning down for his wine glass and finishing it in one gulp.

"I've no idea."

He walks to the window, staring out at Manhattan as the sun sets, the golden light making him appear godlike and invincible, even though he's just a man. He stands there silently, staring out at the city, and it occurs to me that this is the second time the subject of Ireland has come up, and the second time he's withdrawn.

"Ian," I say to his back. "Why did you leave Ireland?"

He's gilded in the light of the setting sun, and I wonder what it will take to break through the veneer gold that cloaks him, to see what's going on in his head.

When he turns around, his eyes are flat. "My glass is empty. I'll go grab the bottle."

Before I can stop him, he heads for the kitchen, leaving me wondering at the mystery of his last days in Limerick and the circumstances that led to his immigration.

***

"They're darling," I whisper, peeking into the tent in Carina's room to find her asleep next to Dylan, forehead against forehead, under a hot pink princess blanket.

"Two peas in a pod," says Ian, his face soft as he squats down to gaze at our sleeping babies.

Dinner ended hours ago with hot fudge sundaes and two once-hyper kids have now passed out.

"Don't wake him," I say, putting my hand on Ian's arm as he reaches out to rouse his son. "Leave him."

"I can't leave him here all night," he says, sliding his eyes to mine. "He'll be disoriented when he wakes up."

"Not if you stay, too."

His eyes widen as he stands up to his full height and looks down at me. His voice is low and taut when he asks: "Is that an invitation, princess?"

It's been a long time since I've had a man between my legs, and after splitting two bottles of wine with Ian, I'm feeling flirty. My inhibitions are down. Not to mention, my body is buzzing with desire for this man. He's hot and I'm willing.

"Why not?" I purr.

He tilts his head to the side, his expression thoughtful, almost wary. "Lots of reasons."

"Like what?"

"You." Gently, he tucks a flyaway strand of hair behind

my ear and a shiver ripples down my spine. "I explained why I couldn't meet you that night, but we haven't really talked about *you*. About how *you* felt. You must have been hurt…and confused."

"It was a long time ago," I tell him, pushing away the memories of that night. Why the hell would I want to talk about the worst night of my life?

"You told me you have trouble trusting people," he continues, "but you didn't that night. You trusted me, and I let you down. You also said you haven't cared about any of your lovers… and your marriage to Steve wasn't exactly typical. I can't help but wonder if—"

"—if one night, fifteen years ago, impacted me so much that it changed the person I am? You give yourself a lot of credit," I say with a smirk, but my words are a defense tactic. He's dangerously close to the truth about how much that night, and his actions, affected me.

"I'm not trying to be big-headed, Tina. I just want to know who you are." He shrugs. "There's no rush. We have time."

"Shhh. Come with me," I whisper, taking his hand and leading him down the hallway from Carina's bedroom to mine.

His words are making something deep inside of me pull and tighten in a way that feels terrible, when I just want to feel good. I don't want to remember that night in Limerick. I don't want to remember the weeks and months that followed, when I was so frightened of becoming pregnant, all the while feeling duped and used. If anything—and maybe especially with Ian—I want to chase the memories away. And sex has always been an excellent distraction from reality. Why should this time be any different?

I push the bedroom door shut behind me and lean against it. Standing a few feet away from me, he crosses his arms, staring at me in my moonlit bedroom.

"Here we are," I whisper, toeing off my shoes, ready to get started.

"Did you ever think we'd meet again?" he asks, persisting with these fucking questions that are making me feel edgy and vulnerable and uncomfortable, churning up long-suppressed feelings of worthlessness. "Did you ever think about me? Because I thought about you. About us."

The word "us" is like a dagger through my heart, so I ignore it, stepping toward him. I clasp my hands behind his neck, rubbing my body against his. "Kiss me, baby."

He stiffens at the endearment, lifting his chin to keep his lips out of reach from mine. "Did you, Tina? Did you ever think about us?"

"Stop talking," I tell him, trying unsuccessfully to keep the edge out of my voice. I arch my back and feel my nipples hardening, pressing against his chest through his dress shirt. "Kiss me, *baby*."

"Don't call me that," he growls.

"How about 'lover'?" I murmur.

"Don't call me anything," he says, getting frustrated with me. "Just talk to me, Tina."

Shut up!

Something inside of me, not unlike molten lava heating up inside of a volcano, is starting to bubble and pop.

"No. No more talking," I say, my fingers curling at the nape of his neck.

"Please," he begs me softly.

"No!" I yell, jerking my head back to look up at him as my nails dig into his skin. "I don't want to talk about it. I don't want to remember how I felt that night or all the nights that came after. Just *fuck me*, Ian!"

He flinches, his eyes searching mine, angrily at first, then softening by degrees. Finally, he reaches up and takes my hands, gently removing them from his neck, but holding my wrists tightly.

"I'll not fuck you like a stranger, *macushla*."

Embarrassed, both by his rejection and because he's called me out on wanting detached, emotionless sex, my body flushes with heat. "Why not?"

"Because you're not a stranger to me."

I'm furious with him. Livid. I struggle against his grip, but my wrists remain shackled in his hands.

"Fine!" I snipe. "It's all fate! That's what you want to hear, right? Thanks for bringing us back together, universe! Now, fuck me, Ian!"

He shakes his head. "No, love. Not like this."

"Fuck you!" I cry, trying to turn my nails into the flesh of his palms. The cage around my heart, that's kept it protected for years, is starting to fail. It can't contain the overwhelming rush of memories, which are as fresh and painful now as they were fifteen years ago. "Let me go!"

"No to that too," he says firmly. "I'll not fuck you, Tina, but I won't let you go either."

Without warning, he whips me around and pulls me back against his chest, holding me tightly from behind as I fight and flail with the hoarded fury from my betrayed and heartbroken teenaged self.

"Fuck you!" I scream again, locked in his embrace, struggling like hell to free myself from his arms. I kick my legs and my bedside lamp goes careening to the floor, the lightbulb shattering on the hardwood.

My bedroom door opens and Gaspare peeks his head in. "Is everything all ri—?"

"GET OUT!" I bellow. *"Leave us alone!"*

The door quickly closes and my fight resumes, but I am losing on all fronts.

I am back in that hotel room again, checking the clock every five minutes, staring out the window for a glimpse of him, my pussy still tender from our lovemaking the night before. It's seven o'clock...eight o'clock...nine o'clock...ten o'clock...and little by little, I'm dying inside. I was used. I'm a stupid, gullible little girl who gave up her precious virginity to a boy more than willing to take it without a backward glance.

"I thought you *cared*!" I spit through gritted teeth. "I thought it *meant* something!"

"I did," he says evenly, like my writhing body doesn't even faze him. "And it did."

"No, it didn't!" I yell. I'm furious and I want him to be

furious too, but he stays calm and part of me hates him for it. "It didn't mean anything!"

He grasps me tighter. "Yes, love. It did."

I am weeping uncontrollably, tears spilling down my cheeks, my breathing ragged as I try to catch my breath against gut-wrenching sobs. "You *never* came back! You *didn't* love me! You didn't mean *any* of it! You *used* me and left! What a good joke to fuck a stupid princess! You didn't care…you didn't care…you didn't care…"

"Get it all out," murmurs Ian, in the same voice I use when Carina has a tantrum or a nightmare. "Get it all out, love, and then we can move forward."

"It meant *n-nothing*! You meant *n-nothing*!" I'm no match for his strength and I feel my body going limp against him as my fury, flowing from my body like boiling poison, starts to cool. "*I* meant *n-nothing*!"

"You meant everything," he says, his arms around me unrelenting.

"*F-Fuck you*," I sob, giving up the fight.

"You're okay, now, darlin'," Ian whispers near my ear, pressing his lips gently to the tender skin of my neck. I savor his touch. I want more. I need more. *Please.* "You're okay."

My throat is raw from crying, and the muscles that tried to fight him ache. He turns me around and holds me against him, my body flush against his, and rests his lips on the top of my head as I burrow into his chest and cry. He lifts me easily in his arms and sets me down on my bed. As I weep softly, he lies down beside me, his front to my back, his arm anchoring me to the solid strength of his body. I put my hands over his, clutching him to me, clinging to his warmth and strength after years and years of loneliness.

I don't know how long it takes, but little by little my tears subside, until I am spent and still beside him. And only then—nestled safely within the harbor of his arms—do I finally sleep.

***

If there is anything more therapeutic than having an emotional breakdown fifteen years in the making, I don't know what it is. When my eyes open the next morning, it's like a thousand-pound weight's been lifted from my shoulders.

I know who's beside me, and I remember our confrontation last night. I unleashed hellfire on him, even though what happened between us in Limerick wasn't his fault. I guess a decade and a half of pain was too much to be reasoned with. But what sweet relief to finally express it and let it go.

Turning slowly in his arms, I face him, my nose a breath away from his, my lips as close.

He is a breathtakingly beautiful man: strong and masculine, scarred and stunning. That unruly curl I remember so fondly droops softly over his forehead, and my heart swells with so much tenderness, I almost can't bear it. My feelings for him, long dormant, rise up within me, so much more than chemistry or attraction, but not translucent enough to be given a name. I only know it feels good to be with him again. So very, *very* good.

"Good morning," he rumbles, though his eyes remain closed.

"Good morning," I whisper.

"Before I let you go…are you going to take a swing at me?"

"No," I say, leaning forward to nuzzle my nose gently against his. "I'm better now."

He peeks at me from under thick, dark lashes. "Sure?"

I nod. "I'm better, but don't let me go."

His lips tilt up as his eyes close again. He readjusts his arms around me to hold me securely against him. "Whatever you say."

Staring at his face—at the whisper of a dark beard shading his jaw—I realize how little I actually know this man. I knew him for one magical night when we were young, and our unexpected reunion has reignited that spark. It's exciting, yes, but daunting too. Who is he? And how does adult-Ian fit together with adult-Valentina—if at all?

Today—this very moment—is day one of a second chance for Ian and me. I don't want to mess it up, but I'm not exactly skilled at relationships. I'm not sure what happens next.

"Tell me something true, *caro mio*," I say, closing my eyes and breathing him in. "Anything."

"*Caro mio*," repeats Ian, his voice wistful. "You called me that. That night."

And no one since, my heart whispers, allowing myself to feel something *real* for the person lying next to me in bed.

After so many years of forcing myself to bottle up my emotions, I savor the experience of feeling, of falling, of *allowing myself* to fall for someone.

"Something true? Hmm." He nuzzles my nose. "I care about you."

"You barely know me."

"My smile knows yours," he murmurs. "My heart remembers yours. My ears long for the sound of your voice. My body wants yours as much as it ever did."

Part of me wants to get naked and jump him for saying something so sweet and sexy, but I'm trying to make a point, so I press on.

"What's my favorite food?" I ask him.

"Hmm." His eyes open again, narrowing in concentration. "Chocolate."

"Everyone's favorite food is chocolate." I try again. "What did I study at university?"

He takes a deep breath and sighs. "I have no idea."

"Art history. What did you study?"

"Business," he says, grinning at me as he warms up to my game. "What's my favorite drink?"

"Beer," I answer, taking a guess.

"Correct. And yours?"

"Prosecco," I say.

"You don't prefer real Champagne from France?"

"It's too dry. I like a little sweetness."

"Me too." He nods. "How many kids do you want?"

I giggle softly because there's something so intimate about the question that it's foreign to me. But then again, here we are, lying in my bed, our bodies clothed but flush, with a very *intimate* part of him prodding against a certain *intimate* part of me.

"More than one," I answer softly. "God willing."

"Me too." A shadow falls across his face. "I loved having a brother."

"I wish I'd gotten to meet Albie."

"I wish you had, too. He was a great kid." He pauses, then asks. "You have a brother, don't you?"

I smile at him. "Do you remember Nico?"

"I never met him," says Ian with a lazy grin. "But he covered for you that night, so I already like him."

"He's married now. He and Bella live in Switzerland."

"I've never been."

"I figured," I say, remembering his reluctance to talk about Ireland last night. I lean up on my elbow, looking down at his handsome face, something inside of me that was long broken now rebuilding itself. "Won't you tell me what happened? The real reason you left Limerick and haven't been back?"

His brows furrow and one of his hands unclasps me as he rubs his jaw. "I can't."

"Why not?"

He shakes his head. "I promised someone."

"But you can trust me," I tell him.

"I *do* trust you," he says. "But I…"

"You don't," I say, sitting up and crossing my arms over my breasts. "We barely know each other, and you don't trust me."

I know I'm being a brat, but I can't help it. I've had a lifetime of self-imposed deprivation and loneliness; now that its cage is gone, my heart wants to make up for lost time.

He sits up beside me, elbowing me gently. "We know each other a lot more than barely and I trust you more than anyone except Craig and Brenda."

"Your American relatives."

He nods, which feels evasive. Unless I know what happened in Ireland, I'll never truly understand Ian. And I want to know him. I want it more than anything.

"If I asked you yes and no questions could you answer them?"

The look on his face tells me he doesn't like this game, but he nods his head slowly. "Go ahead and ask."

"Did something bad happen to you after your brother passed away?"

"Yes," he answers, averting his eyes from mine.

"Immediately after?"

"Yes."

"And it landed you in the hospital?"

"Yes."

"And you *had* to leave Ireland?"

He nods. "Yes."

"Can you ever go back?"

"No," he whispers. "I won't."

Without another word, he turns away from me and swings his legs over the side of the bed. "Kids'll be up soon. How about I make breakfast?"

I want to reach for him—to rub his back or place a reassuring kiss on his cheek—but he's already leaving my room by the time I say, "Okay."

***

His mood is markedly improved as he flips pancakes for Carina and Dylan half an hour later, my little girl looking up at him with stars in her eyes.

I could get used to this.

As I sip coffee at the kitchen table, grinning at the three of them standing by the stove, I decide that it's okay for us to unfold slowly to one another. We found each other, we are reunited, and we want to know one another again. Those are important steps. The speed and depth at which information is traded from now on doesn't have to move at light speed. There is joy in slowing down, in not rushing. We can move at any speed we like; having enough time isn't an issue for us anymore.

"Princess."

Gaspare appears beside me in his usual fleet-footed manner, and I start, looking up at him. "Good morning, Gaspare! You surprised me."

He bows slightly. "Apologies. I was wondering if I could have a word?"

"Of course."

He glances at Ian and the children. "In your study, madame, would be better."

I notice that Iago stands behind Gaspare, his expression grim as he stares at Ian, who adds two more pancakes to a stacked platter on the counter.

"Alright." I stand up and call over to Ian, "I'll be back in a minute."

His eyes twinkle when he grins at me. "Don't be long or there won't be any left!"

I chuckle softly as I leave the kitchen, headed to my office. Once there, I take a seat at the desk once used for business by Steve's father, and Gaspare closes the door behind him.

"What's all this about?" I ask him.

"Your new...friend." He takes a deep breath and sighs as he sits down in a guest chair across from me. "Mr. Prince."

"I expressly told you to leave him alone!" I cry, banging my palms on the desk for emphasis. "Really, Gaspare, I am—"

"His name isn't Ian Prince. It's Ian *Ladd*. And he's a criminal."

I blink at him, my breath catching. "What?"

"He shot a man. Fifteen years ago."

"What? You're...lying!" I reach up and press my hand over my racing heart. "What are you *talking* about? What are you trying to—"

"Coincidentally, you were actually in Ireland when it happened, madame. Do you remember going to see a play in Limerick during a European tour? *Romeo and Juliet*, I think."

I nod.

"It happened the following night. Mr. Ladd shot a man named Jack Murphy."

"He...*shot* someone?" My voice sounds too breathless, unfamiliar.

"Yes, indeed. Then fled the country."

My mind flashes back to the incident in the Limerick alley and I know, without a doubt, that this new information relates directly to that confrontation.

Can you ever go back? I asked him this morning.

No, he answered. *I won't.*

All of the pieces fall into place.

Jack threatened me.

Ian beat him up.

But, Albie. How does Albie fit into this?

Was Ian's brother truly hit by a truck? Or was Albie killed in retaliation for his beating? I suck in a sharp breath, drawing my own conclusions.

Albie wasn't hit by a truck, I decide.

Jack killed Albie.

And Ian shot Jack.

Oh, God. Oh, sweet Jesus.

This terrible chain of events started with me. *I* decided to wait for a boy in a dark alley. If I hadn't made that decision, Ian's brother might still be alive today.

My eyes fill with tears, and I wince with pain as the impact of my actions—the terrible result of my foolish and impulsive teenage behavior—ripples across time to horrify the adult I am now.

"Is he dead?" I ask, my voice a shredded whisper. "Jack Murphy?"

Gaspare shakes his head. "No. He lived, no thanks to Mr. Ladd."

"So, it wasn't murder," I murmur, feeling weak with relief.

"Well, it was certainly *attempted* murder. I'm sure you will agree that we cannot trust him around you or *la bambina*." Gaspare clears his throat, his expression imperious. "I will take care of this. I'll remove him from your home, and we'll make it clear that he's not welcome here. I can even call the authorities in Ireland and let them know—"

"You'll do no such thing," I hiss at him. After my part in his misfortunes, Ian deserves my understanding and compassion, not to be thrown out of my house like a common criminal. "You expressly went against my instructions not to look into Ian's history, Gaspare. I couldn't have made myself clearer on the matter!"

"Anything I do, I do for you, Valentina!" he cries, pressing his hands over his heart in a way that makes me deeply uncomfortable.

His eyes flare with passion, and he looks like a lover, not a bodyguard. Add to this, I have never given him permission to call me by my Christian name. It's deeply inappropriate that he should do so, and tells me that his feelings for me have surpassed those deemed suitable between an employer and employee.

"I'm relieving you from your duties," I say quietly, sorry to say the words to a once-trusted servant, but also recognizing that they're probably overdue.

"No! On what grounds?" he demands.

"For direct insubordination," I say, keeping my voice level and as calm as possible under the circumstances. "Find somewhere else to stay for the next few days. I'll be in touch when and if my anger cools."

"Princess," he says, his jaw set in anger and his eyes flinty. "I have lived my whole life *devoted* to your service. Devoted to *you*!"

"If you have any interest in retaining a position in my household, you need to leave *now*," I say firmly.

I stand up, but he stays seated.

"*Out, Gaspare!*" I bellow. "*Now!*"

Gaspare stands up quickly, turns around and leaves my office without another word.

I sit back in the desk chair, taking a halting breath and letting it go slowly.

Oh, Ian. I am so sorry.

I fight back my tears. I have no right to them.

I picture Ian as the sixteen-year-old boy I remember and my heart clutches as I imagine the series of events *I* unknowingly set in motion. I have unintentionally wronged this man in ways that should be unforgivable, and yet he's standing in my kitchen right now, making pancakes for my baby, after spending last night absorbing my anger; all to clear the way for a future between us.

If that isn't love, my heart whispers, *I don't know what is.*

I stand up from my desk and lift my chin.

I have contacts all over Europe, and the combined clout of the Trainor and De'Medici names is real.

I don't know the statute of limitations on attempted murder in Ireland, but I will use all of the resources at my disposal to help Ian and clear his name. It's the least I can do to make amends.

CHAPTER 9

Ian

I noticed Valentina's beady-eyed bodyguard whispering to her at the table, then watched them leave the room. A few minutes later, he stalked back into the kitchen, spoke a few words to the other bodyguard, gave me a hard look, then left.

I have no idea what's going on, but I don't have a good feeling about it.

While the kids eat pancakes perched on stools at the island in the center of the kitchen, I keep flicking my eyes to the foyer where Valentina disappeared. When she finally reappears, her face is bleak and her eyes, which were filled with such joy earlier this morning, are shadowed. She glances at me, then bites her bottom lip and looks away quickly, plastering a fake smile on her face as she approaches the kids.

"Mmm! It smells delicious!" She leans down to plant a kiss on top of Carina's head, then slides effortlessly to Dylan and does the same. "How was breakfast, *bambinos?*"

"Yum," says Carina, "my tummy is so full!"

"My daddy makes the best pancakes in the whole world," Dylan informs her.

"I think you both need some fresh air and exercise!" says Valentina, looking at her daughter's bodyguard. "Will you take them up to the playground, Iago? Mr. Prince and I will join you in a little while."

"Are you su—"

"*Now*, Iago," she says, brooking no further argument.

"Of course, madame," he says, giving me a disgusted look before ushering our children out the front door.

Tina stands at the counter with her back to me, her platinum blonde hair pulled up in a messy bun, her yoga pants and rumpled t-shirt unexpectedly sexy because everything about this woman turns me on.

"Tina," I say, my voice gruffer than usual, my nerves taut and hackles up. "What the fuck is goin' on, then?"

When she turns around, her eyes are brimming with so many tears, I don't know how she's keeping them from falling. The only thing I know for sure is that I must comfort her, because I cannot bear to see her this sad. I pull her into my arms, holding her against me, worried when she struggles to free her hands but relieved when she winds them around my torso, hugging me back.

"What happened?" I whisper, rubbing her back as she shudders, quiet sobs accompanying the tears that are wetting my undershirt.

When she doesn't answer, I swoop her up into my arms and carry her to the couch in the living room. Settling her on my lap like a wee one, I press her head against my shoulder as she weeps.

"You're scarin' me, Tina," I murmur, pressing my lips

to her soft hair. "Please talk to me, love."

She takes a deep, ragged breath, and I get the sense that she's trying to calm herself, to regain control over her emotions. Finally, after a few sniffles, she leans up, looking at me with bleak, bloodshot eyes.

"I'm...s-so...v-very...s-sorry," she manages to sputter before more tears trickle down her cheeks.

"For what, love?" I ask her, reaching up to cup her cheeks, using my thumbs like windshield wipers to swipe her tears away.

She clears her throat, her eyes holding mine with so much sadness, so much regret, it's carving a bloody hole in my heart.

"Why?" I whisper.

"I know why you left Limerick," she says softly, tears still streaming down her cheeks.

My lips part, dropping open in surprise, and my hands slide down her cheeks until my knuckles rest by my hips on the couch. I tilt my head to the side, desperate to explain how I came to shoot a man, but unable to find the right words. Even now, after all these years, my thoughts and feelings about shooting Jack Murphy are so complicated, I can barely explore that chapter of my life without a full bottle of whiskey nearby.

I'm furious with myself for not killing the bastard.

Relieved beyond measure that he lived.

Angry for letting down Albie.

Unable to regret the night I spent with Tina.

And frustrated that I cannot find peace.

"You sh-shot Jack Murphy," she says softly. "The night you d-didn't come b-back."

"Yes. I did." There's no point in lying. She knows. Maybe she even has a right to know.

"And it's m-my fault."

Of all the things I might have expected her to say next, this is not one of them. I flinch, my neck whipping up so my eyes can find hers. "What? No. No!"

"If I hadn't w-waited for you in the alley that n-night, n-none of this would have h-happened."

"That's not true," I say.

"It is," she insists. "You fought J-Jack for me. Jack k-killed your brother. You shot Jack. That's why you've n-never been able to go home. I r-ruined your l-life. *I* k-killed your b-brother!"

More rough than firm on account of my emotions, I pull her against me, holding her tightly as my own eyes fill with tears for the first time since the morning I discovered my brother was dead. She throws her arms around my neck, burying her face against my throat, her sobs and short, jagged breaths ripping my heart to shreds.

"It's not yer fault," I whisper near her ear. "I promise you, darlin', it wasn't yer fault. Not even a bit."

"It all s-started because of me," she sobs.

"No, darlin'. It started when the Clancys and Keegans and Murphys and Doyles got into it decades before either of us was even born. Limerick was always a powder keg waitin' to explode. It had nothin' to do with you. Nothin' at all. I promise you on me mam's grave, love. You're innocent in all of this."

"How can you bear to l-look at me?" she asks, leaning her head up from my shoulder to find my eyes. She is still crying, her beautiful face blotchy and her lips quivering.

"Because I don't blame you," I tell her, cupping her cheeks again.

I lean forward, pressing my lips to hers for the first time since finding one another again. She tastes like coffee and salty tears, and I don't know how, but I manage to be gentle with her despite my raging need for her. She twists in my arms a little, pulling my neck down so that I can kiss her better. My tongue slides between her lips, sweeping into her mouth, and she moans softly, a hum that I feel on the velvet underside of my tongue. She is pliant and sweet, needy and hungry, and if I don't stop kissing her now, I'll be inside of her in another minute.

Nuzzling her nose tenderly, I finally lean away, breathless and undone.

"I don't regret our night together," I tell her, wincing as I contemplate the truth I've always known. "God strike me dead, but I wouldn't give it up for everythin' that came after."

Her face crumples as she turns into my chest, wetting my shirt all over again. "H-How can you s-say that?"

"Because it's true," I tell her. "Because you were the brightest light my dark life had ever known. Because I didn't know what *beauty* was, what *love* was, what was *possible*, until I met you. Because when God sees fit to place an angel in your life, you don't ask how much it'll cost."

"Even if it costs your brother?"

"Ah, love. God took Albie for His own reasons. But in His mercy, He also gave me you."

"Do I belong to you?" she whispers, her voice awestruck and hopeful.

When she looks up at me, cradled in my arms like a treasure, our eyes lock together. Hers are as dark and deep as black coffee, brilliant after crying, and framed with wet lashes. But these are the same eyes that have haunted my dreams for a decade and a half, from which my soul has never wandered, for which my heart has searched in vain. They are before me once again, and I will do anything to keep them before me forever.

"You tell me," I say, my heart skipping beats, my voice as hopeful as hers.

"I want to belong to you," she tells me, her lips drawing closer and closer to mine until they finally brush together when she adds: "I want you to belong to me."

When we kiss again, it is with the knowledge that tragedy and love can happen at the same time; that you can meet the love of your life on the same night you suffer an almost unbearable loss. And maybe that's not fair, but that's life, in all of its terrible and beautiful authenticity. And it's *our* journey—hers and mine, for better or worse—and for that reason alone, I wouldn't trade it.

I scoop her into my arms and stand up, kissing her mindlessly as I walk from the living room to the foyer and down the hallway that leads to her bedroom. After laying her gently on the bed we shared last night, I undress quickly, and she does the same.

Her body is warm and soft against the hard angles of mine, but when I sink into her, into the divine, wet heat of her sex, the quivering muscles hold on tight; not unlike our hearts, which held out hope for all these years—which never really gave up on each other, despite harrowing odds against us.

When I come, hard and fast, my seed flooding the hidden depths of her sweet body, my throat opens in a primeval roar, and my lips cry out for the world to hear:

"You are mine!"

And I am hers.

I love her. I have always loved her. I will love her until I die.

No matter what happens in this life or the next, I know the truth at the very core of my existence; the fuel that propels my very being forward through this life:

My love for Valentina De'Medici is everlasting.

***

Valentina

I've read that lightning can and will strike the same place twice, even decades or centuries later, which is why, I suppose, I don't question Ian's sincerity or honesty when he tells me, for the second time in my life, that he loves me.

Love at first sight doesn't happen often, but it *does*

happen, and it happened to us. It's been true since the moment I first saw him in that Limerick theater. Maybe it was true even before that: maybe God made Ian and God made me, and He destined our hearts to find and love each other.

It doesn't matter if the whole world were to tell us it's impossible.

In my love's elegant vernacular:

The whole world can go fuck itself.

It's been a week since I learned of my inadvertent part in Albie's death, but the man I love refuses to blame me, much like I refuse to regret the choices I made that led to Carina's conception. Trading some could mean losing all. Life has led us back to one another, a gift we won't take for granted.

I reached out to the legal team that Steve assembled and considered the best in Europe, and asked them to look into the shooting of Jack Murphy. Promised some clarity on the situation by today, I keep glancing at my phone as I walk to the Yellow Magnolia Café to meet Ian and the children for lunch. They attended a special children's event this morning with Brenda, who treats Carina with the same mother-hen kindness that she bestows on her adopted grandson, Dylan. With my parents and Nico far away, I'm grateful for the feeling of extended family afforded to us by the Princes. My life in Brooklyn is richer than I ever could have imagined.

When my cellphone buzzes with a European country code, I take a seat on a bench and answer the call, crossing my fingers that Ian's name can be cleared of any crimes and he can, if he chooses, return to visit the land of his birth.

"Hello?"

"Mrs. Trainor? This is Graciela Turot from the Trainor International legal department. I have some news for you."

"Yes, Graciela. Go ahead."

My heart thumps painfully behind my ribs.

"As you know, The United States and Ireland have an extradition treaty in place," says Graciela, "so if Mr. Ladd, aka Mr. Prince, was wanted for a crime committed in Ireland, any notification to the authorities of Mr. Ladd's whereabouts could prompt an extradition hearing, leading to his arrest and deportation."

"Mm-hm. But I asked that you be very subtle in your inquiries, Graciela," I say sternly. I certainly didn't want to get Ian in *more* trouble. I just wanted to know where things stood legally, and how—or *if*—I could help.

"And we were, ma'am," she assures me, "but a Mr. Gaspare Vizier—formerly in your employ, I believe—had already tipped off the Irish authorities as to Mr. Ladd's location upon our inquiries."

"What?" I gasp in shock, which quickly morphs to fury. I fired Gaspare several days ago, unable to keep him in my employ, knowing that he'd always be suspicious of and combative with any man I chose to invite into my life. "Gaspare called the police?"

"He did, ma'am. As soon as we asked about Jack Murphy, the authorities in Limerick mentioned that they'd had a call earlier in the week about the shooting, and were aware of Mr. Ladd's presence in Brooklyn, New York."

I gulp, trying to hydrate my dust-dry throat.

Dio Mio! Are they coming for him? Are the NYPD on our heels as I sit here talking? Should we go into hiding? I will do whatever it takes to keep Ian safe, to keep him from seeing any time behind bars.

"What should we do?" I ask, my voice quavering. "What happens next? Will there be an arrest? Extradition?"

"Well, that's the interesting thing about this case," she says. "Upon further conversation with the Limerick police, we learned that charges were never filed against Ian Ladd. Not at the time. Not ever."

"What?"

"We had our source in Limerick comb through outstanding warrants, but there wasn't one for Mr. Ladd. In fact, the report made by Mr. Vizier earlier this week is the only known report of a shooting by Ian Ladd. There were other petty crimes committed by Mr. Ladd on record, but those precede the shooting of Mr. Murphy, and most were filed under juvenile mischief."

"But will they open a case now? Based on Gaspare's tip and your inquiry?"

"Actually, ma'am, that's the best news of all and the real purpose for my call. The statute of limitations on assault with a deadly weapon in Ireland is only six years. And since this 'supposed' crime took place over fifteen years ago, Mr. Ladd couldn't be arrested or extradited now, even if Mr. Murphy *chose* to make a complaint. Too much time has lapsed."

"So you're saying…"

"That Mr. Ladd is not a wanted man. Anywhere."

Oh, yes, he is, I think to myself, a smile blooming across my face as my heart takes flight. *He is wanted very much. Right here. With me.*

"He's safe," I whisper.

"Absolutely," says Graciela, "and free to travel back and forth to Ireland at will."

"Thank you," I tell her. "Thank you so much for looking into this for me."

"Of course, ma'am. It's our pleasure. Feel free to call us at any time."

"Goodbye."

"Goodbye, Mrs. Trainor."

When I stand up, I tuck my phone into the back pocket of my jeans, and run-walk to the café with wings on my heels, eager to share my news with Ian—to let him know that the slate is finally clean, and he can come and go, wherever he likes, whenever he wants.

A small crew of people I love stand by the front door, the children's hands in Brenda's, while Ian stands nearby with a picnic basket.

I wave to them all, kissing Carina, Dylan, and Brenda's cheeks before tilting my neck back so that Ian can press his lips to mine. Our children giggle, but I think they like seeing Ian and me together—Carina assured me last night that although she'll never call Ian "Babbo," she will find another special name for him.

"Brenda said she'll take the kids to lunch," says Ian, winking at me. "She packed us a picnic."

I'm so touched by this gesture, when I turn around to thank her, I end up kissing her again. My own mother is a distant, cool and aloof presence in my life; Brenda's warmth and thoughtfulness is a welcome contrast to such a rigid upbringing.

"Go have a picnic, young lovers!" she says with a chuckle, herding the little ones into their favorite restaurant with promises of ice cream, and leaving Ian and me alone.

"Have a spot in mind?" I ask him.

"My favorite spot?" he suggests. "In the rose garden?"

I grin and nod, taking his hand as we stroll in the direction of the roses, taking our time, enjoying the fact that—as Ian pointed out last weekend—there's no need to rush our courtship this time.

"I have news today," I tell him. "Good news."

"Oh, yeah?" he asks, smiling down at me. "Tell me, then."

"Well, I had the legal team at Trainor International look into, you know, what happened with Jack Murphy and—"

He stops walking. "You did what?"

Suddenly, I'm uncertain. "Did I do something wrong?"

"No. No, love," he says. "I just...I didn't know you were worried about that. The statute of limitations on assault is six years."

"I know," I say, staring up at him. "You can't be extradited."

"Not that Jack Murphy ever pressed charges. He didn't," adds Ian. "He knows he beat up Albie and sent him to his death."

"So, you already knew," I say, tilting my head to the side.

"Sure," he says. "I've known for years. I just didn't have permission to share the details with you…until today. I talked to Gene, Brenda, and Craig. They said that if I trust you, they trust you too. I can tell you anything you want to know."

"As long as you're safe," I say, looping my arms around his neck and standing on tiptoes to kiss his lips. "I don't need to know anything else."

"I'm safe," he says, kissing me back.

"You're mine," I tell him.

"That I am, lass."

We kiss again before he takes my hand and we continue our stroll toward the roses. But I'm reminded of something that's not adding up: when Dylan asked to go to Ireland, Ian said no. And when I asked if he could return to Limerick, he said he couldn't.

"You *can* go back," I say. "You *could*. If you wanted to."

He pulls me under the white-painted pavilion, where roses clamber up lattices and hang across arches and cascade down ladders, all second-chance flowers, all in the second flush of bloom.

"But I don't," he insists, setting the picnic basket down on the ground so that he can cup my cheeks tenderly. "I won't ever. Limerick is my past. Brooklyn, here with you, *macushla*, is my future."

Dio Mio, I think, before his lips touch down on mine and all decent thoughts are whisked away, *may it be so*.

EPILOGUE

One Year Later

Ian

Sixteen years since I first laid eyes on my princess, and a year since our reunion in New York, I stand across from her in the Cranford Rose Garden, under a bough of second-flush roses.

Just behind the young Catholic priest from the progressive, neighborhood church we attend together, is Albie's bench. My brother is with us in spirit, if not in flesh.

Between us, under our clasped hands, are Dylan, a handsome ring-bearer, and Carina, a lovely flower girl.

Tina's sister-in-law Bella, who traveled from Switzerland with Nico, is her matron of honor, and Craig, dressed up in his Sunday finest, stands behind me, my best man.

Smiling at us from a row of white chairs are Nico, plus Brenda and her brother, Eugene, who's come all the way from Ireland to witness and celebrate our union. It was a surprise to see Dr. Trímian after so long, but Tina's reassurance that what happened with Jack Murphy is no longer a liability to Dr. Trímian made him more comfortable about attending.

Though we've lived as husband and wife in Tina's loft for the better part of a year, recent news that we're expecting a baby prompted us to make everything official. Dylan and Carina will have a little brother at Christmastime; a little one we plan to name Romeo.

There are some that might be stumped as to how one of the richest, most beautiful and sophisticated royals in the world ended up married to a scrappy Irish restaurateur in Brooklyn, but that's only because they don't know our story:

Once upon a time, long ago and far away, in a magical city by the River Shannon, a street rat fell in love with a beautiful princess…

…at first sight.

THE END

A NOTE FROM THE AUTHOR

Dear Reader:

You will no doubt recall, from the 1992 Disney-version of "Aladdin," that most of the action between Aladdin and Jasmine happens in three (very brief!) acts:

The first is the magical night when they meet on the streets of Agrabah;

The second is when Aladdin arrives at the palace under the guise of Prince Ali Ababwa to pursue Jasmine's hand;

And the third is when Aladdin returns to the palace one final time for his showdown with Jafar and to proclaim his love for Jasmine not as a prince, but as himself.

Plotting these three acts into a semi pre-written narrative about the Italian princess from *Shear Heaven* was challenging, as was finding room for Abu (Albie), the Genie (Eugene Trímian), the Sultan (Steve), and wicked troublemakers, Jafar (Gaspare) and Iago (Iago.) There were times I wasn't sure I'd be able to pull off an updated modern version of "Aladdin" with any finesse…which is why it took three years longer than planned to publish.

But now that it's finished, *At First Sight* is one of my all-time favorite novellas. How I've loved seeing my Aladdin (Ian Ladd/Prince) and Jasmine (HSH Princess Valentina Yasmina De'Medici) thrust into the familiar story-scaffolding of such a beloved fairytale, complete with the happy ending they both deserve. I hope you will find it similarly enchanting!

With so much love to all of my fans and readers, both loyal and new,

Katy

xoxo

** PURCHASE MORE OF KATY'S FAIRYTALES HERE **

The Vixen and the Vet
2015 RITA® Finalist
2015 Winner, The Kindle Book Awards
(inspired by Beauty & the Beast)

Never Let You Go
(inspired by Hansel & Gretel)

Ginger's Heart
(inspired by Little Red Riding Hood)

Dark Sexy Knight
2017 Finalist, The Kindle Book Awards
(inspired by Camelot)

Don't Speak
2017 Silver Medalist, International Book Awards
(inspired by The Little Mermaid)

Shear Heaven
(inspired by Rapunzel)

At First Sight
(inspired by Aladdin)

For announcements about upcoming a modern fairytale releases, be sure to sign up for Katy's newsletter at **http://www.katyregnery.com**!

AT FIRST *Sight*

ALSO AVAILABLE
from Katy Regnery

a modern fairytale
(A collection)

The Vixen and the Vet
Never Let You Go
Ginger's Heart
Dark Sexy Knight
Don't Speak
Shear Heaven
At First Sight

THE BLUEBERRY LANE SERIES

THE ENGLISH BROTHERS
(Blueberry Lane Books #1–7)

Breaking Up with Barrett
Falling for Fitz
Anyone but Alex
Seduced by Stratton
Wild about Weston
Kiss Me Kate
Marrying Mr. English

THE WINSLOW BROTHERS
(Blueberry Lane Books #8–11)

Bidding on Brooks
Proposing to Preston
Crazy about Cameron
Campaigning for Christopher

THE ROUSSEAUS
(Blueberry Lane Books #12–14)

Jonquils for Jax
Marry Me Mad
J.C. and the Bijoux Jolis

THE STORY SISTERS
(Blueberry Lane Books #15–17)

The Bohemian and the Businessman
The Director and Don Juan
Countdown to Midnight

THE SUMMERHAVEN SERIES

Fighting Irish
Smiling Irish
Loving Irish
Catching Irish

THE ARRANGED DUO

Arrange Me
Arrange Us

ODDS ARE GOOD SERIES

Single in Sitka
Nome-o Seeks Juliet
A Fairbanks Affair
My Valdez Valentine

STAND-ALONE BOOKS:

After We Break
(a stand-alone second-chance romance)

Braveheart
(a stand-alone, suspenseful romance)

Frosted
(a stand-alone romance novella for mature readers)

Unloved, a love story
(a stand-alone suspenseful romance)

Under the sweet-romance pen name
Katy Paige

THE LINDSTROMS

Proxy Bride
Missy's Wish
Sweet Hearts
Choose Me
Virtually Mine
Unforgettable You

Under the paranormal pen name
K. P. Kelley

It's You, Book 1
It's You, Book 2

**Under the YA pen name
Callie Henry**

A Date for Hannah

ABOUT THE AUTHOR

New York Times and *USA Today* bestselling author **Katy Regnery** started her writing career by enrolling in a short story class in January 2012. One year later, she signed her first contract, and Katy's first novel was published in September 2013.

Several dozen books and three RITA® nominations later, Katy claims authorship of the multititled Blueberry Lane series, the A Modern Fairytale collection, the Summerhaven series, the Odds Are Good collection, the Arranged duo, and several other stand-alone romances, including the critically- acclaimed mainstream fiction novel *Unloved, a love story*.

Katy's books are available in English, French, German, Hebrew, Italian, Polish, Portuguese, and Turkish.

Check out Katy's Website: **http://www.katyregnery.com**
Sign up for Katy's newsletter today: **http://eepurl.com/disKlD**

Made in the USA
Middletown, DE
21 June 2020